Dedalus Eu
General Editor: Timothy Lane

Baltic Belles:

The Dedalus Book of Estonian Women's Literature

The Editor

Elle-Mari Talivee was born in Tallinn in 1974.

Elle-Mari Talivee, PhD, is a scholar, critic and writer. She divides her time between her posts as a project manager at the Estonian Literature Centre and as a researcher at the Museum Department of the Under and Tuglas Literature Centre.

The Authors

Betti (Elisabet) Alver (1906–1989), one of the greatest Estonian masters of poetic style, made her debut in 1927 writing short stories, and she published a short novel *Tuulearmuke* (*The Wind's Paramour*) shortly after. Her first poetry collection appeared in 1936 and made her a renowned poetess. A freelance writer, she became the member of the Estonian Writers' Union in 1934. Her marriage to the poet Heiti Talvik can be described as one of smouldering inspiration. Talvik died in a Soviet prison camp in Siberia, after which Alver's literary voice fell silent for a long time as she translated works by Pushkin, Gorky, Goethe and Heine into Estonian instead of writing original works. Her short stories and poems that began to appear again after 1965 are both brilliant and intense.

Elisabeth Aspe (Elisabeth Nieländer, 1860–1927) was one of Estonia's first realist writers. The daughter of a small-town miller, she graduated from a high school for girls. Aspe lived briefly in St. Petersburg but wrote her main works at her childhood home in the 1880s. Influenced by the female German authors of the time, Aspe wrote works that are marked by a longing for the wider world and the conflicts between rural and urban life. Her female characters are usually women who expect fate to make their choices for them, but feel at the same time a need to manage life on their own. Aspe's novel *Ennosaare Ain* (*Ain of Ennosaare*, 1888) was one of the first depictions of a university-educated Estonian.

The Authors

Aimée Beekman (b 1933) is a professional camerawoman, the author of fifteen novels, and a prolific travel and children's writer. She became a freelance author in 1960 after working in the Tallinn film studio. Beekman's novels published in the 1970s contain feminist qualities that were frowned upon in Soviet society. One of the more interesting themes that surface in her works is the mundane tragedy of a passive individual whose problems and difficulties often turn grotesque. Beekman's novel *Valikuvõimalus* (*Option to Choose*, 1978) has been made into a film.

Maimu Berg (b 1945) has worked as an editor, critic and columnist, and has also been a politician. She has translated several works into Estonian, primarily from Finnish. Her novel *Ma armastasin venelast* (*I Loved a Russian*, 1994), which smashed through taboos and has been called the Estonian *Lolita*, has been translated into several languages. Berg's novel *Moemaja* (*Fashion House*, 2012) was inspired by her long career as a fashion magazine editor. The author's vibrant and liberal works, which consider the possibility and impossibility of love, offer a fascinating take on history. She often writes about the Soviet era. Her 2017 collection of short stories *Hitler Mustjalas* (*Hitler in Mustjala*) includes a host of brilliant alternative histories; in one of them Angela Merkel visits Estonia in search of her roots.

Maarja Kangro (b 1973) is a translator, poet, librettist and short-story writer, with a master's degree in English philology. Kangro published her first novel in 2016, the jarring semi-

The Authors

documentary work *Klaaslaps* (*The Glass Child*), which has already been translated into German and Latvian. She has translated philosophy and poetry from English, German, French and Italian. Kangro's powerful writing is one of the most compelling examples of contemporary Estonian prose. Her short story *Fireworks* was published in *Best European Fiction 2018*, the annual anthology of contemporary European literature.

Viivi Luik (b 1946) is an author of poetry, short stories and essays. Her novel *Seitsmes rahukevad* (*The Seventh Spring of Peace*, 1985) is one of the most influential Estonian works of literature, in both its style and its subject matter. As the wife of the diplomat and writer Jaak Jõerüüt, Luik has lived in Helsinki, Rome, New York, Riga, and Stockholm. Her novel *Ajaloo ilu* (*The Beauty of History*, 1991), which deals with events surrounding the Prague Spring, has been translated into fourteen languages, including English (2007). Luik's novel *Varjuteater* (*Shadow Theatre*, 2010) is a memoir-like travelogue of a lifelong journey to Rome.

Helga Nõu (b 1934) fled with her family to Sweden in September 1944. A writer with a long career in teaching, she has been active in the Estonian PEN Club and was in the now-defunct Foreign Estonian Writers' Union. She lives in both Uppsala and Tallinn. Nõu's novels convey various important issues for refugees, especially inter-generational conflicts and the difficulties of trying to integrate into a new society. She has written extensively for youth, exploring society's tender spots without ever lecturing on morality.

The Authors

Eeva Park (b 1950) made her debut as a poet, but has since published four collections of short stories. Her parents were both writers. Her needle-sharp, portrait-like novellas often weave together Soviet-era memories and tribulations with those of today. Her novel *Lõks lõpmatuses* (*A Trap in Infinity*, 2003), which delves into the topic of human trafficking, has been translated into several languages. Park's 2016 novel *Lemmikloomade paradiis* (*Pets' Paradise*) suggestively tells about a writer's "imprisonment" in an Irish castle and her liberation through writing. Her poetry collection *The Rules of Bird Hunting* was published in English in 2018.

Lilli Promet (1922–2007) was a prose author with a fascinating visual style. Promet's novel *Meesteta küla* (*The Village with No Men*, 1962) dissects that experience. Promet made her writing debut in Leningrad in 1944, where she was sent during the siege of the city to work for Estonian-language radio. Promet was a professional writer. Scripts adapted from her short stories gave rise to four Estonian films in the 1960s. The perimeters of Soviet literature couldn't quite manage to confine her entirely either, and the German-language translation of her novel *Primavera* (1971) was later removed from bookshelves in East Germany.

Asta Põldmäe (b 1944) is an author and translator who has written for both adults and children. She has had a long career in journalism and has worked as an editor of Estonia's most prestigious literary journal *Looming* since 1986. Põldmäe's lyrical prose is an exceptional voice in Estonian literature, as she is a perfectionist of language and style, and she treads the

The Authors

fine line between genres. As a translator into Estonian, she has worked primarily with Spanish and Finnish texts.

Mari Saat (Mari Meel, b 1947) is a Doctor of Economics and a Docent of Business Ethics at Tallinn University of Technology. Saat writes both novels and short stories in a quite unique, psychological prose with a keen sense of society. Her novel *Lasnamäe lunastaja* (*The Saviour of Lasnamäe*, 2008) was published in English translation in 2015. Saat has also written for children and has published a business ethics textbook. She often focuses on the variety, complexity, and conflicts of everyday life. Saat's writing is characterised by sensitive insights into the human psyche, symbolism, and the weaving of fantasy and reality.

Elin Toona (Elin-Kai Toona Gottschalk, b 1937) fled with her family from Estonia in 1944 and has since lived in England and America. Toona has written literature in Estonian about the problems faced by second-generation refugees abroad; in English, she has written radio plays, novellas, monologues, articles, and short stories. Her autobiographical novel *Lotukata* (1969) was published in English as *In Search of Coffee Mountains* (1977; 1979). Her memoirs titled *Into Exile: A Life Story of War and Peace* (2013) was selected as one of *The Economist*'s books of the year, and was awarded a prize by the Cultural Endowment of Estonia in 2018.

The Translators

Adam Cullen is a freelance translator of Estonian prose, poetry and drama into English. His published translations include works by Tõnu Õnnepalu, Mihkel Mutt, Rein Raud, Jürgen Rooste, Veronika Kivisilla, Asko Künnap and Indrek Hargla. He is a member of the Estonian Writers' Union and on the board of its Translators' Section.

Eva Finch studied English language and literature at Tallinn University. She has over twenty years' experience as a translator from English to Estonian, her native language. Eva translated the classic novel *Toomas Nipernaadi* for Dedalus with her husband Jason Finch. She also organises cultural exchanges between Finland and Estonia at the Estonian Centre in Turku, Finland.

Jason Finch is a native speaker of English, an academic researching and teaching English literature of the modernist era in Britain at Åbo Akademi University in Finland. He has also published on modern Estonian literature. In the past he has worked together with Eva Finch to translate miscellaneous texts from Estonian to English. They translated *Toomas Nipernaadi* for Dedalus.

Christopher Moseley was born in Australia in 1950 and is a freelance translator into English from Estonian, Finnish,

The Translators

Latvian, and the Scandinavian languages. He has translated numerous Estonian short stories and three novels, one of which is *At the Manor*, or *Jump into the Fire* by Maarja Kangro. He currently lives in the UK and teaches Estonian and Latvian at the School of Slavonic and Eastern European Studies, University College London.

Contents

Foreword	17
Ain of Ennosaare by Elisabeth Aspe	31
The Wind's Paramour by Betti Alver	40
Family Tree by Aimee Beekman	51
The Seventh Spring of Peace by Viivi Luik	63
Ella by Elin Toona	91
Lying Tiger by Lilli Promet	98
In the Eye of the Wolf by Helga Nõu	103
Tango by Eeva Park	115
In the Winds of Blue Heights by Mari Saat	131
The Bolide Shard by Asta Põldmäe	152
Awakenings by Maimu Berg	182
At the Manor, or Jump into the Fire by Maarja Kangro	205

Foreword

Women in Estonia could enrol in any school of higher education in the Russian Empire from 1915 onwards and achieved suffrage in 1917. The February Revolution toppled the Russian Empire's Romanov dynasty, which controlled the territory of Estonia at the time, and set the stage for the proclamation of Estonian independence in 1918. The University of Tartu, which was founded in 1632 and was Estonia's sole university at the time, had by then already admitted over 500 women as students.

However, the desire of women to gain the right to education dates back much earlier. In 1887, Lilli Suburg (1841–1923), a female writer and schoolteacher, founded *Linda* as the first feminist magazine in Estonia. Lydia Koidula (1843–1886), Estonia's first great patriotic poetess and a symbol of its national awakening, received the highest possible education a woman was allowed at the time in a high school for girls. She passed an exam in 1862 at the University of Tartu and was granted a certificate allowing her to work as a governess. The University of Helsinki began accepting female students in 1870, and some courageous young women travelled much farther. In 1902 a young teacher Minni Kurs began her studies as an external student of political sciences at the University of London, where she became a close acquaintance of Emmeline Pankhurst. Back in Estonia, she published articles on women's rights.

Foreword

Estonian literary history meanwhile shows that female Estonian authors had already asserted their presence by that time. Lydia Koidula worked alongside her father as the editor of a large newspaper, and was also the founder of Estonian theatre. Koidula (a pen name that alludes to the dawn in Estonian) published fiction as well as poetry inspired by the folk-music traditions of Estonia. Her writing was heavily influenced by German and Russian literature. As one of the first women authors in Estonia she undoubtedly became a role model for the other female Estonian writers that followed.

The epigraph before a chapter by Elisabeth Aspe (1860–1927), the first author in this anthology, directly alludes to Koidula's influence. As the eldest daughter of a family living on the edge of Pärnu, a summer resort in southwest Estonia and at the time an important port for the flax trade, Aspe was raised to take over her father's mill and business. As a young author, she had a "room of her own". After she married a businessman, her creative activity unfortunately dwindled, and following his death, she took over his business and his debts, and the task of managing the whole family. The excerpt in this selection from her short novel *Ennosaare Ain* (*Ain of Ennosaare*, 1888) reveals the musings of an old farmwoman on Martinmas, or Saint Martin's day, also known as Old Halloween. The story is set during the Estonian national awakening in the mid-19th century, and the hardy Estonian woman weighs the chances of finding her stepson a strong and industrious wife. After a day of hard work, Aspe's character Peet also visits the schoolmaster's house, hungry for knowledge. The short novel debates the unusual dual Estonian-German identity of the protagonist, and how romance brings him to return to his

Foreword

national roots. The slightly romantic, early realist literature reflected the influence of German literature, such as the novels by E. Marlitt published in the newspaper *Die Gartenlaube*, which was widely read across the German speaking world, and the conservative Baltic German view of gender roles. But Aspe managed to blend her own life experience with ideas from the national movement into her stories.

In 1900 the Estonian folklorist Oskar Kallas married the Finnish writer Aino Krohn (1878–1956) and took her to live with him in his homeland. Estonia thus became Aino Kallas' "country of fate". Although she wrote in Finnish, she was utterly fascinated by her new home and its history, and also by the fate of the women of the country. Oskar Kallas was appointed Estonia's ambassador to the United Kingdom in 1922 and as a result, many of Aino Kallas' short stories were published in English, her 1924 first edition had a foreword by John Galsworthy. Her novellas, which significantly affected and broadened the Estonian literary tradition, are also counted among Finland's literary treasures.

At the beginning of the 20th century the issue of feminism was raised by Kallas and by Estonian women authors who were directly involved in the 1905 Russian Revolution. That revolution laid the foundations for the creation of the Estonian Republic in 1918 but it was put down by the authorities and its leaders were convicted or managed to escape into exile. The question of women's rights arose together with the idea of the modern woman from the young revolutionaries, and the revolution itself has left a trace in several epic Estonian novels set in the beginning of the 20th century. Perhaps though, one of the most romantic results of that process is the short novel by

Foreword

Betti Alver (1906–1989), one of the most outstanding Estonian poets of the 20th century, who began by writing prose. Alver's short novel *Tuulearmuke* (*The Wind's Paramour*), which she wrote as a schoolgirl, won second place in a 1927 Estonian novel-writing competition and remains unsurpassed in its depiction of the spirited melancholy of youth. The work is like a piano piece, with the protagonist Lea, a young pianist studying at the conservatory, playing variations on that piece of music. The young generation then lived and studied in the city, but their roots were in the countryside; Lea's are in her home village, which is situated between the bogs and the sea. She catches the eye of a doctor whose late wife looked exactly like her but was selfless and mild-mannered, unlike the lively young Lea. A conflict arises in which she must make a choice and decide whether to lose herself or to turn down the love she is offered. Similar independent and self-reliant personalities often feature as ideals in Alver's poetry too. When the Republic of Estonia was established, Estonian women got equal civil and political rights to those of men, but socially and economically a married woman was still under her husband's custody.

Lea, Alver's protagonist, comes from a fishing village on the coast of the Baltic Sea. As this collection moves chronologically through Estonian literature, hints of what Estonian village society might have been like before the Second World War can be gathered from the excerpt taken from Aimée Beekmann's (b 1933) novel *Sugupuu* (*Family Tree*, 1977), the second in her *Coppertown trilogy*. The novel's rich assemblage of characters is connected by the slightly mythical and ancient Estonian village of Coppertown (Vaseküla) in the

Foreword

first decade after the First World War. There, the elderly woman Jaava has been the heart and soul of an age-old farmstead, and after her death, her eleven children from two marriages come together to grieve. The loss of their mother and grandmother, the main pillar of their world, causes them to peer deep into their own souls; Grandma Jaava had been known as "Satan's daughter" around the village. Aimée Beekmann herself was among the writers who started to publish in the 1960s, and some of her novels are female *Bildungsroman* focusing on the psychological growth of a woman. Her female protagonist often challenges the traditional family ideal. Feminist topics began to appear in Soviet Estonian literature in the 1960s and 1970s, and the private sphere, marriage and extramarital relationships were then often the centre of novels. Though popular, these novels were not considered to have any literary value. It was ideologically mandatory for the Soviet woman to be equal to the man, working as a tractor driver or labourer, and her self-realisation was directed into the public sphere, not towards the family or any private life. This meant she had a double burden, as women also took on all the domestic duties, which were not considered appropriate for men to do. It is interesting that Soviet Estonian women authors have often brought forward the feminine qualities of their heroines as they try to find a way to play the role of a woman; this in itself almost constituted dissident behaviour.

In the first part of the 20th century many Estonian artists, writers and musicians, men and women, went to Paris to study and work in the capital of the arts. Lilli Promet's short story *Lamav tiiger* (*Lying Tiger,* 1964) describes the yearning for home felt by the Estonian artist Eduard Wiiralt while

Foreword

he was living in Paris (one of Wiiralt's pictures is featured on the cover of this collection). The tiger being sketched is perplexed by the Nordic flora that surrounds him, and the trees that grow in the homeland that the artist dreams of. Promet was herself the daughter of a painter and studied ceramics, and as a result, she often depicted scenes involving artists using collage techniques. This miniature is typical of her way of telling a story in general, showing her love for detail, the depth of feeling, and a softness that is not so common in the Soviet literary discourse. Lilli Promet (1922–2007) knew the meaning of homesickness well. She experienced the difficulties of war behind the Soviet lines during the Second World War, at Tatarstan and at the siege of Leningrad.

***

This anthology also touches upon the deportations and forced exile of tens of thousands of Estonians in the middle of the 20th century. The Republic of Estonia was occupied by the Soviet Union in 1940, and this was followed by Nazi occupation during the war and then the return of Soviet occupation in 1944.

Viivi Luik's (b 1946) novel *Seitsmes rahukevad* (*The Seventh Spring of Peace*, 1985), which the Soviet censors probably allowed to be published by accident, received resounding praise at the time. The protagonist in the novel, a little girl living in a rural Estonian village that was devastated by the war and by the Stalinist Soviet regime, is a character upon whom all the torment and fear of her surroundings is projected. The bleak picture spans the autumn of 1950 through

Foreword

to the spring of 1951 and conveys a world of farms emptied by deportations, abandoned fields, men lost in the war, and Forest Brother partisans hiding out in the forests. This novel reflects through the eyes of three generations the experience of the post-war world where men do not dominate, as the little girl is mainly cared for by her mother and grandmother. Although this world is sometimes conveyed with childish brutality, it is a fragile place full of fleeting shadows. Viivi Luik, who is also a poet, uses highly poeticised language, and the contrast between the horror of the time and the way it is conveyed creates one of the most outstanding Estonian novels.

The excerpt included here of the writing by exiled writer Elin Toona (b 1937) is the opening of her book *Ella* (2008), which she dedicated to her grandmother. As a young child, Toona fled from the horrors of the war together with her mother and grandmother. The grandmother, Ella Enno, had already been helping to raise young Elin in Estonia, and she continued giving her lessons about both her former home and her new one, firstly in the displaced persons' camp in Germany and later in England. Ella's grandmother, who had a passion for art and literature, was married to the Estonian poet Ernst Enno (1875–1934), whose biography Toona has also written.

In the Estonian-language cultural journal *Tulimuld*, which was published by Estonian refugees in Sweden, Toona once compared the protagonist of her novel *Lotukata* (*In Search of Coffee Mountains*, 1969) to the girl in Luik's *The Seventh Spring of Peace*: "Two children from opposite shores. One in occupied Estonia, the other in occupied Germany. Both are free souls held in captivity. We see the worlds of these two seven-year-olds through their own eyes like a securely-framed

Foreword

landscape. The war separated them politically, ideologically, and geographically, but their landscapes are almost identical. The frames are made from the same materials: fear and unfeeling, insurmountable regimes."

Toona balances mesmerisingly on the line between autobiography and novel. The narrator of *Ella* is the prototype for her character in *Lotukata*, which translates as "little Kate with the funny hat". The author has remarked that she only became a true refugee when her grandmother died. Toona, as a female writer, often mediates very directly the experiences of a girl or a woman. As with Luik and *The Seventh Spring of Peace,* the storylines in both *Ella* and *Lotukata* are about three generations of women having to cope in the tough conditions of a post-war world without men.

The novel *Hundi silmas* (*In the Eye of the Wolf*, 1999) by exiled writer Helga Nõu (b 1934) tells the story of Tiina, an Estonian woman who fled wartime Estonia with her family and grew up in exile in Sweden. She endeavours to find herself and define her own identity, spurning the diasporal Estonian society one moment and the opportunities her new homeland presents the next. Tiina ends up dating a Swede, but has a backroom abortion to escape becoming a single mother in a society of exiles where that is sternly frowned upon. The wolf in the novel's title is not just a wolf, but a werewolf.

The werewolf itself is highly symbolic in Estonian literature. In the tragic play *Libahunt* (*The Werewolf*, 1911) by the writer August Kitzberg, one of the founders of Estonian drama, a freethinking young woman named Tiina, who is a social outcast regarded by the community as an aberration flees the maliciousness of others to live in the forest, where she

Foreword

is slain by a bullet from her beloved. The writer Aino Kallas mentioned earlier also created a character named Aalo, who transforms into a werewolf at night on the Estonian island of Hiiumaa. Nõu's novel cites Clarissa Pinkola Éstes' *Women Who Run with the Wolves*.

The intergenerational conflict of *In the Eye of the Wolf* provides space for the strains of womanhood to erupt in physical form, no matter whether the individual in question is genuinely a werewolf or merely "the madwoman in the attic".

***

Eeva Park (b 1950) regularly features female characters and views the world from a strongly female perspective. Park's characters tend to be fearless and unyielding, unlikely ever to lose their sense of dignity, and they rarely leave revenge untaken. A semi-ironic observation of Soviet-era Tallinn unfolds in Park's novella *Tango* (2006), which is set during a time when the most prevalent word was undoubtedly "deficit". Park's main character in *Tango* has come to Estonia from another republic of the Soviet Union, and her depiction of the city of Tallinn is spatially fascinating, observed from the lofty heights of its upper Old Town as if it sits in the palm of a hand and through the critical eye of an artist and an outsider. The French pop star Mireille Mathieu, whom the protagonist meets in the story, was one of the very few Westerners whose music was permitted in the Soviet Union, and who furthermore actually performed in Estonia.

Estonia regained its independence from the Soviet Union in 1991. Soon afterwards the country was rocked by a major

Foreword

catastrophe at sea. The excerpt from Mari Saat's (b 1947) novel *Sinikõrguste tuultes* (*In the Winds of the Blue Heights*, 2000) deals with the sinking of the *Estonia*, a cruise ferry on its way from Tallinn to Stockholm in September 1994. The greatest tragedy ever to happen at sea in peacetime, the incident has been recorded in the literature of different countries around the Baltic Sea. In Saat's work, the novel's protagonist is a young Estonian leatherworker from a suburb of Tallinn who bids *bon voyage* to her Swedish husband on that fateful September night. Her worldview is an exceptionally poetic reflection of the fragility of life, as she is so sensitive to her environment that she seems to have no protecting skin at all. She is in her origin an embodiment of the Estonian nation's jumbled historical background, as her father is Russian, while her husband and the father of her child is Swedish. A small country beside the sea, Estonia is inevitably a crossroads of nations, or even "a windswept land; a geographical prostitute," as Aino Kallas once wrote. Here lies also the argument with those who narrowed the question of the nation to the growth of the population and the role of a woman in reproducing the nation.

When women ask questions, they often have a very different perspective to that of male authors. Asta Põldmäe (b 1944) is an especially sensitive author. In her short story *Boliidi kild* (*The Bolide Shard*, 2010) a university lecturer, who is a solitary man, develops a relationship with a rather moody chip of a bolide, a piece of a meteor. The author mentions Tõravere Observatory, which is also known as Estonia's southern space centre, though it does not keep count of bolides. Estonian literature possesses other traces of majestic shooting stars

Foreword

though, and in a sense the shadow of a comet has hovered over it since 1976. In that year Lennart Meri, the future president of Estonia, wrote his tremendous work *Hõbevalge* (*Silverwhite*), which is a sweeping reconstruction of Estonian and Baltic Sea history that focuses on the Kaali meteorite, which struck the island of Saaremaa about 4,000 years ago. Põldmäe paints wondrous pictures and conjures fairytale-like situations in her poetic short prose, something about which she has theorised from the perspective of a translator and literary critic. Põldmäe has remarked that a short story must have a fast-paced beginning, writing "[It must] begin with the strike of a gong," and "A short story must function like a heart: without skips in the beat."

Maimu Berg (b 1945) tends to be outspoken and mercilessly forthright when exploring the female perspective. Berg's novella *Awakenings* (2015), published in this collection, won the Friedebert Tuglas Award in 2016. Since the beginning of her career there is always something playfully surprising about her novellas and novels. She writes with direct frankness about fears and desires, and the attempts at self-realisation by her characters. Her female character is often beautiful, self-confident and living alone, and *Awakenings* is an example of an upside-down story of Pygmalion.

Thinking about Berg's role in the process of Estonian female prose, it is easy to build a bridge from her to the bold, erudite, and often ironic female perspective of the next generation of young Estonian writers in the 21st century. These members of the first generation that grew up in a newly independent Estonia often see themselves as citizens of the world, and undoubtedly feel it necessary to create a better

Foreword

world in their own country. The piece by Maarja Kangro (b 1973), *Mõisas ehk Hüppa tulle* (*At the Manor, or Jump Into the Fire*, 2014), is full of social-critical humour and shines a harsh light on injustice and prejudice, but at the same time she frequently scrutinises the experience of "making it" as a woman in a society where this is not the norm. This sometimes requires a woman to demonstrate strength and prove herself, something that is not commonly expected of men. Nevertheless, the female characters in Kangro's works are still feminine in essence, and sometimes more fragile than might be expected. Kangro's descriptions are painted with warm sympathy and a hint of tenderness, as well as with black humour. Her characters are often childless and cynical; they suffer pitfalls that must be addressed, but which are commonly taboo or regarded as better not discussed. Maarja Kangro is a human rights activist. This has been one of the important roles played by Estonian female writers, and portraying independent women who are more and more sure in their own choices.

Since 1971 the clear point of reference for the short story in Estonia has been the Friedebert Tuglas Award, which was established by the author of the same name whose works went beyond the boundaries of genre. Several of the authors included in this selection – Betti Alver, Mari Saat, Asta Põldmäe, Eeva Park, Maimu Berg, and Maarja Kangro – have won the prize, some of them multiple times.

Cover image by Eduard Wiiralt

Ain of Ennosaare
Elisabeth Aspe

> *Yet strangely an ancient tale*
> *still tread softly o'er the land:*
> *your people were free before,*
> *and Estonians once stood their ground*
> *upon their northern soil.*
> *(Lydia Koidula)*

It was only Martinmas, but the cold had laid a strong lid over the river and had long since hidden the summer grass trimmings under a white blanket of snow. The wind whined and bleated outside, rattling the little four-cornered window of the Ennosaare farmhouse, rustling in the thatched roof, and howling at the door, as if it wanted to duck out of the cold and into the warm interior. But Ennosaare was inhabited by a young, sedulous man who would not tolerate holes in the roof and had stuffed moss tightly into the gaps between the logs well before, and by a flinty grandmother who had shuttered the doors and windows against the cold. She was alone in the house today, as the children had gone off this way and that to take part in the Martinmas traditions. At dusk, she heated the stove for a second time that day, ventilated the room from smoke, then made sure to shut all the doors tight. Presently, she was seated on a low stool in front of the fire. The stub of a stave torch burned smokily in its holder, casting a tremulous light through the large space. The horses, gathered around a trough in the adjoining threshing room, whinnied and stamped their hooves against the hard clay floor, and every now and then, a drowsy, feathery chicken or two would cluck a household lullaby in their indoor coop. The old woman sat upon her stool didn't want to spin wool on "dear Martinmas", but neither was she seeming to make any progress with the knitting needles she'd fetched from the back chamber. Ultimately, she let her hands settle into her lap, her thoughts semi-consciously drifting into the past. Her hair had gone quite gray since the day her daughter-in-law flung her domestic rights and duties at the old woman's feet and left to serve at the manor house. As if that had come as any surprise! The old woman's youth was over by the time it happened, and eight or nine years of toil and worry aplenty had rolled by since. Life had certainly been difficult with two people away from the work and chores at the same time. The household hadn't seen much of the master's hand, but at the same time, they had no girl to send to the manor to perform peasant duties – something that should have happened after the master's death, and for which they would have had to hire another farm hand. And the mistress of the house! Good heavens: had the old woman or any other housewife ever pulled off such a foolish trick? Up and leaving in the middle of the most hectic harvest time, just like a hired drifter! The child might certainly benefit from it: rumour had it he was being tutored by the baroness' brother! Well, fine: she still wouldn't have let anyone but Peet become master of the house – a man as big as he, with a face and manners like those she'd seen in the men of Ennosaare before, and Peet was the fourth she'd seen! The old woman looked up and scanned the room with a warm gaze, as if having a vision. She'd never had children of her own, but she'd never felt regret ever since Peet came into the world. She'd held that child dear and coddled him more than anyone else in her own particular way. He was also the reason why she hadn't lifted a finger when Mai left with their son. Good riddance! It brought peace to the household. The small amount of extra work – that, she could manage, of course. In her younger days, she'd been a bold, hard-working woman praised all around the parish; one unrivalled in the fields. Back then, her family would say: Watch out when that woman gets a hold of a scythe: you'll have to mow at such a speed that "your eyes go white" so as not to fall behind. And how strong and strapping she'd been! The old woman smiled as she thought back to the good old days. At Villem's wedding at Maidla farm, where she had been the young man's principal singer and had danced in a thick coat all day, the groom's younger brother Mart vowed that he would dance with the young woman of Ennosaare for as long as it took for water to seep from the coat. And the rascal kept his word, whirling her around the dance floor all day long and making her nearly breathless from exhaustion. But had it done any harm? Not a fingernail's worth! Her chores hadn't gotten any harder in the days that followed and over time, the household had prospered. But look at it now! The old woman fetched another long stave torch from above the stove, lit it in place of the smoking stub, which she extinguished, then sat back down in front of the fire. Her thoughts wandered on: nowadays, she often felt fatigued – now, she could use a daughter-in-law to shoulder the yoke of domestic chores. The idea had already crossed her mind long ago, in truth, and at quarrels all around (the folk of Sauga Parish called weddings, feasts, and every other antithesis of peaceful everyday social order a "quarrel") where the young people gathered in one place, she had been on the lookout for a suitable partner who just might stand out – just like at the big wool-spinning gathering at Vanasalme farm lately, where nearly half of the parish women were together in one place, young and old alike. She'd savoured Rõõt of Vanasalme's warm beer that contained plenty of honey and bits of white bread, making her head buzz a bit and even causing her to go and drop a hint or two in regard to the farm's oldest daughter Miina. But what could you do with that Peet of theirs! He could be talkative and smart beyond any other, but at other times was as dull and bewildering as a plank. She certainly raised the topic and elbowed him when he arrived at the dance later that evening, but someone who fails to notice simply fails to notice. He went and chose some lass – one so young she hadn't been confirmed yet – out from the back of the crowd, danced and talked to her alone the whole night long, and everyone witnessing it was already raising their eyebrows and old Leenu of Tiiduoja, whose sharp tongue was unflagging in finding something to say about others, was already whispering this and that. And if only the girl had been someone's respectable daughter. But no: she was a relative of Riin of Papisaare, who had a farm across the river, whom the woman had taken in out of mercy when the girl's parents were evicted to cover a debt for borrowed grain and died soon after in another man's cramped sauna building. But such was the way of those men! If only Peet's father himself had listened when she forbade him from going off to the manor to take a wife…

The old woman lifted her head and cocked her ear. What was that thumping noise rising around the house? Had the rest of the household arrived?

"Dear old granny of the house, dear old grampy of the house," a Martinmas beggar called from outside, "will you let us speak to you? May Martin's beggar enter in?"

Instead of granting permission, the old woman tiptoed over to the door, and she latched it. She wasn't in the mood to receive Martinmas beggars while home alone, or to start handing out the best of what she had, all their bread and meat. She curtly replied: "You may not – go somewhere else!"

Well, it was still light outside and a refusal such as that was quite unexpected to the waiting Martinmas beggars, so the whole crowd began to berate her. While the woman was still weighing up what to do, one of the more zealous of the bunch found that the door of the side space by the threshing room gate had been left wide open and led his companions inside, all wearing their coats backwards and sporting wisps of tow on their jaws as beards. Dancing, they jostled their way up to the old woman, singing mockingly as they did: "Mart leaps about on juniper legs, Mart bounds about on bear legs; Mart came to bring good cheer, to gladden up who's stingy!"

"Sing nicely," a man in a furry coat suddenly barked – one who was several heads taller than the rest of the bunch and appeared to be their leader. "Otherwise, I'll send you all away myself!"

They obeyed at once. The Martinmas "mother" sat down in front of the fireplace to spin yarn, the Martinmas "father" ebulliently proclaimed blessings for a bountiful crop, and the "children" danced and sang long songs about the cold and a silver path through the heavens, sweet black Martinmas pudding, and many other things – just as ancient tradition called for, and all accompanied by a bagpipe. When many a song had been sung and the old woman still wasn't getting up to fetch the shed key and bring treats, the tall man, who up until then had been standing quietly and merely observing the scene, stepped forward again. "Well, dear granny," he prompted her, "where are the sweets for the Martinmas beggars; where is the precious sip of Martinmas beer?"

"The Martinmas sweets are bog moss; the Martinmas beer's at the bottom of the well," the indignant old woman grumbled under her breath. Nevertheless, as the songs required, she took her keys from their peg and went to the shed to fetch treats for the insistent revellers. She rummaged and deliberated for a long time until she'd gathered up flax, peas, sausages, half a pig's head, a couple of candles, and all else that was customary to give. Thanking the old woman and crowing out all kinds of well-wishings, the Martinmas beggars stuck the items in their sacks and danced out of the room in mirthful song. When all the guests had left the yard, the tall man carefully closed the gate and re-entered the house. Inside, he removed his backwards coat, his tow beard, and his straw hat, and serenely sat by the old woman's side in front of the warm fire. She was surprised to see he was none other than Peet himself, master of Ennosaare.

"I thought you were with the schoolmaster – how did you end up in the company of Martinmas beggars?" the old woman inquired.

"I was with the schoolmaster. However, on my way home, I bumped into a group of them by chance, and since they're poor children for the most part, and the old mistress of Ennosaare is always so reluctant to hand out alms, I came along as one of them just for the fun of it and intending to be terribly persistent until half a pig's head was produced. I appreciate that you didn't cause me any trouble as far as that was concerned..." The old woman certainly grumbled on about the mockery and the squandering of household goods, but knowing her grandson wasn't any better for it and that, although he had a rather serious temperament, he sometimes tossed a mischievous trick into the mix, she ceased before long, and by the time the farm hands and the servant girls arrived home, she spoke brightly as she served them a warm meal.

Peet had been at the schoolhouse, which he visited frequently. The schoolmaster held him in high regard as an intelligent young man and strove to broaden his horizons as much as possible for an Estonian at that time. On winter evenings, whenever he had the time, Peet would sit in the schoolmaster's house and listen to what the sensible, rather elderly man had to say about life – which is to say what he, a speaker of foreign languages, had read. He also discussed patriotic matters, though not in the form or sense that people do today. The Estonian fatherland was still shrouded by a "long, dark night" and that, which was passed on orally as song and legend from the earlier, better generation and the bygone days of freedom was, and had remained, a dark style of poetry subdued by the Estonians' dulling, backbreaking slavery – a heritage thought fit exclusively for telling children as bedtime stories. A few books had indeed been written in Estonian, but how many of them could Estonians get their hands on, which is to say: Who knew how to read them? The older parish residents could at least read the catechism and the hymnal, but only because they had memorised the books' contents in preparation for the pastor's questions and for the confirmation ceremony itself; luckily, this knowledge remained in their minds, serving as assets of spiritual consolation in life's difficult moments.

The schoolmaster only had a few Estonian-language books, but the assiduous Peet learned more from those few than many a tepid-hearted man did from a great, well-stocked library. Among other titles, the schoolmaster's collection included a couple of issues of Otto Wilhelm Masing's Estonian-language *Peasant's Weekly*. Peet found these to be particularly bountiful springs of joy. The tall, strapping man was brought to the verge of delighted tears over someone having attempted to deliver enlightenment to his poor nation by way of a newspaper – a nation wasting away in languor, and lacking the enlightenment that other nations long since possessed, according to the schoolmaster. And when Peet later heard that the newspaper publisher himself had been an Estonian who lived and studied in the faraway city of Tartu with a few more learned Estonian sons who did not scorn their lowly kindred brethren, but rather acknowledged themselves as children of that nation and wished to work in the name of enlightening their compatriots, his heart was warmed and tears of gratitude streamed from his eyes. He would have soared to them on the wings of the wind; would have shown them care and done them all manner of kindnesses. And yet he could do nothing and knew not what could be done, because all he had studied was farm labour, and his whole life hitherto had been lived upon that small plot of farmland which supplied him with a meagre living, and apart from that, all he'd done was serf's work for the manor.

1888

Translated by Adam Cullen

The Wind's Paramour
Betti Alver

1

Coming back from the conservatory, I spot the same little boy on the boulevard in front of the hospital again. Every day at noon, he is there pacing back and forth with a brown dog, a solemn look upon his face. As he waits he stares up at the building, and at twelve o'clock, a tall man in a gray coat leaves, takes the child by the hand and strolls to the park.

Today, both only regard me with a long, probing gaze, since the first time we encountered one another the child screamed loudly and ran towards me with damp, wide-opened eyes and widespread arms. The man also froze in astonishment, an unconscious question written on his face and a spark of joy in his eyes.

It lasted for only a moment.

A second later, the man's earlier bitterness drew the corners of his mouth downward and a mask of indifference swept across his countenance once more.

Yet a question, a stubborn expectation, persisted in the child's eyes. What was it about my person that could surprise them so? I'd run a little late today and the clock in town was striking a quarter past twelve.

I observe the late-middle-aged man appear in the clinic

doorway and the child run up to him. Leaping over the puddles, he cries out: "You know what, Dad? She hasn't come yet!"

The man descends the steps and says something softly in reply.

The sky has turned overcast and the wind flings intermittent heavy raindrops into my face. Today, the boulevard is lifeless; only a drowsy driver's cart rattles in the distance. A drenched mason's apprentice emerges from the depths of the park, whistling "Someone to Watch Over Me" extremely loudly and piercingly.

The child's name is Gert.

I overhear the man say to him loudly: "No, Gert, we're going home."

But the child obstinately repeats his demand, over and over, his little legs stomping the mud, and tears himself from his father's grasp with all his might.

"Let's just wait for her, Dad – let's wait! She'll be coming any minute, you'll see!"

"Be reasonable, Gert!"

But the pleading voice grows even more insistent.

Then, they notice me. The man clenches the child's hand more tightly and looks away towards the whistling clay-covered boy who has already moved on to "Merry Widow Waltz".

The dog at his left side utters a low growl and bares its teeth.

"Dad, Dad, listen, Dad," I hear the child rattle on behind me, "listen, Dad, can I ask now? I'm going to ask, okay..."

"Watch out for the water! Be quiet, Gert!"

I turn to look in astonishment. Tears stream down the

child's solemn face as he peers up at me from beneath his blue sailor's cap.

Ah, what a curious little button-nosed boy with that tearful twist in his lips!

"What's wrong, little Gert?" is what I would like to ask, but a glance at the glowering man forces me to bite my tongue. Why on Earth doesn't he allow his child to speak, that crabby old moth of a man? I flash the child a smile and turn back around. Gripping my folder of sheet music more tightly beneath my arm, I turn left and walk briskly through the mud.

2

The rain intensifies after lunch and Eva is unable to dispel her boredom. She wraps herself in a long red shawl, pulls her feet up onto the chair, and flips through a spring fashion catalogue.

I come downstairs to practise.

I push Eva's dance music and operetta booklets aside and start tackling a difficult new étude.

"Lea!"

"Yes?"

"Forget that boring exercise for today, I can't bear to hear it! Play something cheerier!... or, better: come sit here at the window! What nasty, nasty weather! Did it really have to go and rain today? We had plans to meet at Monastery Park at five o'clock this afternoon: Inge, Aksel, Ohakas, and I. How foolish, foolish... any of them *could* come here, of course; but no! This weather is driving me mad! You know what, Lea? If this rain doesn't let up, then I will take rat poison tomorrow – I swear it!"

"That's nonsense, Eva! Would you like me to play something from *Dodo*?"

"No. I will take poison, I'm not kidding! I wonder if Mother will still put up a fight about my new coat then! Don't laugh, I truly wish to die! You'll understand once you're my age."

"Sure, sure I will, you old crone! You've been twenty years old for seven days already. Awful."

"That means nothing. I could give it all up right now, everything in this tedious world."

A teardrop falls onto the fashion catalogue. Is Eva really crying? Is today's walk truly worth it?... hmm... is it Ohakas, perhaps?

"Look at what an interesting dress this is, Eva. Pale green silk with coral. If you were to take a walk in Monastery Park wearing it one day, everyone would fall in love with you. Green suits you so well."

"One doesn't go out dressed like that, little lamb! It's an evening dress. Original, indeed! Those folds in the side and the dangling beads... the sound they would make as you danced – absolutely exquisite! And this one here – Oh! That heavy silk with its silver lace – divine! Oh, Lea, darling, this silk coat would suit me *wonderfully*, and a lavender hat such as this – or this mottled one here with the brocade fringe, instead! Hans says I should only ever dress in dark colours, but Harry believes I'm something out of this world in pink. Would you just look at this little hat with the tiny bells! How pretty!" Oh, the bulky catalogue holds so very, very much; so many new and fascinating dresses! So very much of it would suit Eva

– her fair, tousled hair and her smiling eyes that had lost any remaining trace of melancholy.

And that cashmere dress, that athletic wear, that captivating coat!

What would Nata say? What would Inge say if they saw her in that bengaline dress?... Inge's eyes would widen in jealousy and she'd be in a foul mood for days; Nata would sit down on the spot, even in the middle of the street, a look of profound amazement on her kind face.

"And you can only imagine, Lea: Nata thinks she has a classical profile – ha-ha! She always turns to the side when speaking, have you noticed? Once, at a café, one of Grit's colleagues asked me: "Why is Miss Lipov always staring over her shoulder?" And do you know what Hans replied? "Miss Lipov has lost her Greek features and is now looking for them..." Ha-ha-ha! Just think, what a boy! How mad! You hear? She's lost... her Greek features... ha-ha-ha!... that big chin and long, long nose! Oh, I just can't!"

Eva laughs. She laughs so hard that tears spring in her eyes again.

It's still raining outside.

Gurgling streams trickle down the street and the tin-gray scraps of cloud seem to have wrapped themselves around the church steeples. Occasionally, someone holding an opened umbrella passes by through the dusk, leaping cautiously over the puddles and frothing gutters spewing rainwater onto the pavement. Darkness creeps through the room and the clock on the wall ticks unusually loudly.

Suddenly, hurried footsteps sound from the stairs and Inge bursts in, her raincoat dribbling on the floor.

"Children! News!" she calls out, shaking the raincoat and causing drops to fly all the way to the piano. "If you only *knew*!"

Eva has recovered from her laughing spell and stretches luxuriously.

"Ooh!... well, what is it, Inge? Did you meet with Orvik? Hmm?"

"Orvik? Our dearest Orvik will be coming later. But now, first, a cigarette. So. *Fuchs, Feuer*! Kiddies, something damned great is afoot!"

Inge loves to sit higher than others.

She sits upon a chair back and rests her feet on the table. For a few moments, she stares at Eva and me with a promising grin, silent. Then, with great elegance, she lights her unfiltered cigarette, blows smoke through her mouth and nostrils, and coughs a little.

"So: big news! I can't understand how on earth people make smoke rings... what? Patience, I'll tell you. *Achtung*: April 3rd is Aksel's birthday; did you know? Fine. Look, Eva: isn't Lea almost like an embalmed Egyptian princess right now?"

Eva scrutinises me.

"How so? I don't see it."

"How so?... hmm... I don't know, either, but Lea: you're an embalmed princess. I saw one at the cinema once..."

"Alright, Inge," Eva interrupts impatiently. "The news?"

"Fine, listen up then: Hans Grit has written a tragic comedy; a mortal writer's immortal work, as he himself puts it. Or maybe it was the other way around... my God, Eva! Just wait a second! It's a play about a prince and two princesses.

Baltic Belles

The prince arrives at a country where a widowed queen mother lives with two beautiful daughters. One studies ballet, the other is a professor of mathematics. The prince goes to court them with an entourage of his pages, a jester, and a state chancellor, and..."

"It's a fascinating story and all," Eva interrupts, "but Inge, you promised to tell us some kind of news. What happened to that?"

"Be patient, will you?! All in good time! *So*, once again: the prince and his entourage come to find him a wife, and whom does he court?"

"The mathematician."

"The ballerina," Eva guesses.

"Ha-ha-ha, that's the whole thing! Neither of them. He courts the mother. The fat, rich, ugly widow. As for the daughters, the professor marries the jester and the ballerina weds the chancellor. Interesting, isn't it?"

Inge takes out another cigarette and leans over her knees.

Eva stares outside in disappointment and gnaws at her lip. She then yawns deeply a couple of times, pulls her shawl (which in the meantime slipped off) back over her shoulders, and disparagingly remarks: "Foolishness."

Inge smiles superciliously.

"It's *not* foolishness. Hear me out to the end, and then you can say whether it's silly or not. We, *we* will perform it on Aksel's birthday, wearing costumes and wigs; we'll perform it in front of an audience. And do you have any idea whom Aksel is inviting? Go have a glass of cold water first, children! Orvik. Aksel is inviting Jüri *Orvik*, and we will perform in front of him! Did you hear, my little piggies? God, how we will *dazzle* him! We have talent and charm – oh, children, how surprised he will be! Heavens, heavens!"

Inge stands up on the chair, presses her hands to her breast, and shouts, as if Eva and I were deaf: "We have talent, I know it! I have it, at least. And Orvik is divine! Divine, I say! When he wears those green trousers and that lace collar... did you see him in *The Last Candidate*? How he danced, and that look in his eyes as he did... Oh, children! I sat in the second row and I felt as if... Oh, God, I'm going mad! Tell me: you both love Orvik, don't you?"

"Of course I do, Inge!" Eva says, curling up on the chair. "I love him to death. What sort of costume am I to wear?"

Inge strides up to me and sits down on the piano keys, producing a sudden, unharmonious bang.

"How strange it is that all three of us... stop it!" she says, tearing my left hand away. "Tell me, Lea: you do love Orvik, don't you?"

"Me? That clown? Out of my way!"

"What's that? You don't? You don't love Orvik? Woman, woman – you're *insane*! But it will come. I wonder: which of us three will have the most luck?... Oh, children, I can already tell I'll have to cause you both such grief – he always looks me in the eye so queerly – but do not condemn me for it!"

"That's absurd, Inge! He always smiles at me on the street. I saw him at the post office on Wednesday: his gaze followed me the whole way out!"

Inge arches her eyebrow.

"So? Are you saying you have eyes in the back of your head, too?"

Eva bites her lip and is unsmiling.

"No matter. What was, was, but he *did* watch me go."

"That's impossible, Eva! He prefers brunettes, you know."

"You're deeply mistaken. Blondes are his taste!"

"But he smiled at me!"

"You're lying!"

"Eva! Do you really want to deny that…"

The doorbell rings. Auntie has come home. Crossly, she asks: "Another quarrel? Who was smoking here?"

Inge explains something about Aksel, to which auntie shrugs and retires to her bedroom. Inge continues as if nothing happened.

"Here's the cast list: Grit will play the prince, Ohakas the chancellor, and none of them but me are fit to be the jester. They're so awfully stiff."

"But me? Who will I play?" Eva brusquely demands.

"Patience! Lea will be a dancer because of her legs, of course. You will be the professor princess."

However, this didn't appear agreeable to Eva.

"I suppose that's some character in a gray overcoat, a top hat, and glasses? I'd rather have Lea's part."

"Don't try to swap! You'll get a hat with a feather in it, a wig, and corduroy trousers. You can be satisfied."

"But what about Mrs. King?"

"Undetermined as of yet. It must be someone fat and repulsive. Anyone can play her, as far as I'm concerned: Hans and Aksel could get off their arses for once, too. Let them search for someone. I recommended Nata – you know, that… you know her… delicate musical soul… and suddenly she was all up in arms about it. She refused. We don't need a piece of work like her. So: will you two agree?"

"Yes."

"Wonderful. You'll get your scripts on Monday, and Thursday will be the first rehearsal. Do you know what happened at Café Rennert yesterday, Eva?"

Inge launches into a long and winding story about a fresh café scandal.

3

I find two letters upstairs in my room. The first is from my step-brother, written on poor paper and rife with ink blotches and errors:

Dear Lea,

So why don't you write any more? Come down to Turvaste soon! I fixed your bench today, it was quite rotten already. And the posts crooked. I made a new birch seat and hauled sand up from the beach in a wheelbarrow. Tomorrow I'll start painting the boat and will go to Roimarada to fetch new oars. Grandma misses you dearly and her back only ever aches too. Especially before rainy weather. So I'll give her a coat of turpentine and arnica tincture, arnica tincture is better. The thrush nest boxes are already up, the sorrel is limping a little. We bought a new cow in late February. But now we don't know what to name her. What do you think? Lood came over yesterday and told us to christen her Genevieve, but I think he was joking.

Come soon!
Jaan

The other letter is from my brother:

I'll travel as soon as I can. Landscape *won no awards. Send money; no need for reproachful letters.*

Harald

1927

Translated by Adam Cullen

Family Tree
Aimee Beekman

Recently a bad habit of Lilit's had been getting worse: she constantly got lost in her thoughts. Then, standing idly, she occasionally came round with a start and looked round, startled. Fortunately, nobody had so far rebuked her for this inappropriate behaviour, but it was safer if no one's glance fell on her during such a moment of reflection. So it became a kind of habit that, after the afternoon's milking was complete Lilit leaned against the upper bar of the pasture gate, relaxed her legs and stared into the air. The old gelding also had nothing against standing still, the milk churns on the cart. The nag only wanted to hang about; his head jerked down immediately, just like he wanted to warm his achy knee joints with his breath, and the eyes closed. Nodding off like this the gelding used to open his lips wide – goodness knows who the horse constantly showed his teeth to in his geriatric dreams.

Earlier, Lilit had used a yoke to carry the milk home from the pasture, until Johannes stepped in her way one day and started a strange monologue. Out of the blue, he remembered his late wife Eeva, who had toiled away at Villaku all her life without complaining and, even sick, carted Roosi from place to place. Lilit had not understood if Johannes had really come from Lower Rossa to the gate of Villaku pasture, only to tell Lilit about her predecessor! Johannes was not some soppy old person, nostalgic about the past. Lilit had listened to Johannes with concern: was her father-in-law about to lose his marbles? Nothing else was to be heard at home apart from Viida and Roosi's strange talk and Naan's breathing. Lilit had always dashed across the field to Lower Rossa when she needed sensible advice on farming or the household. Had Johannes, Lilit's strong pillar, started to falter in his old age?

Slowly, Lilit had started to realise that Johannes didn't have the courage to come out with his concern directly. Fate had laughed at the Villaku family, anyway, and one must not invoke demons. Johannes was thinking about the future; the Villaku family couldn't stay so small forever. Johannes put his hopes in Lilit and told the young woman to look after herself. Johannes advised her to take on a girl and choose a horse good enough to bring the milk churns back from the pasture. Johannes lit up when Lilit started to nod in agreement with him. Just as if he was thanking her for her sharpness, he started to praise Lilit. He couldn't have done otherwise – everybody wants to be happy with himself at least once in a while; it was Johannes who had found a wife for his son Naan. The whole village was laughing when Johannes brought a wife home for Naan. First, Lilit had feared the neighbours' glances and suffered from their offensive comments. Later the village calmed down and started to respect Lilit in their way. They wondered that the motherless and fatherless Lilit was so diligent and temperate. This praise was not pleasant to hear, either – sweet was mixed with bitter: it was said that wasn't this good-for-nothing Naan lucky, because such loyal and strong-minded women are in short supply.

That time, when the two of them were standing at the

pasture gate, Johannes' words brought the tears to Lilit's eyes, as if it was she who was old and couldn't resist bursts of sentimentality. Lilit had always tried to be sober and sensible – what else could she do – and Johannes' concern shook her. The old man's words touched her heart. She was not used to anybody worrying about her, anybody trying to lessen her work load, thinking about her son and the baby daughter and even her unborn children. Lilit had come to believe that a lucky star had directed her to Johannes; thanks to the old man she didn't have to wrestle alone with life's troubles. It was incredible that a stranger had decided to help the poor girl and pave her path.

That summer's day when the old man had said what he had to say and then disappeared behind the rye field of Lower Rossa, Lilit had seen the Villaku buildings, fields, grove and garden with new eyes. Lilit had thought that this must be what happiness is: having a safe place in the sun. Lilit had the feeling that from now on she could do whatever hard work was required, overcome melancholy when it wanted to grab her, and settle all the quarrels in the Villaku household amicably. With all her heart she had wanted to chase gloom out from under the roof of Villaku – in her joy she believed herself powerful. She had even intended to change Naan; why couldn't that man become strong, brave and talkative? It wouldn't take that much: you only had to find and break the barrier in his soul forcing him to be shy and quiet. If life had turned a warm and friendly facet to Lilit and melted her soul – why couldn't the same happen to others, too?

However, today Lilit was standing at the pasture gate, life rolling on in the same old way, as she debated with herself, as if that conversation with Johannes had never happened, the one after which Lilit had wanted to fly, cheering.

***

Naan was holding Lilit's hand tight, as if thinking that she was scared of the dark and needed a man's protection and support.

Thank goodness, there was no danger now that somebody would pursue Lilit. It is not on to chase after a mother of two. But years ago – Lilit had barely got used to living at Villaku – Naan had once had to take out his gun to protect his wife. In his rage, Naan wouldn't have stopped at anything: he would have shot that man, that's quite clear. You can't accept and give in if someone wants to rob you of the only soul dear to you.

Naan had lived in this world for thirty-seven years when the pastor married him to young Lilit. Better late than never. Naan was lucky to find someone so dear to him. Never would he have thought that a woman can be that dear to a man. It was a miracle of miracles that someone wanted to be close to him, this lump of a man who found it difficult to talk to people and had not been able to make friends even in his childhood.

Abel of Muraka almost met his end. Had he popped up from out of some bush, there would not have been much to say. Then Naan's hand was still steady, just back from the war; there in the trenches every man was able to become one with his gun. At the front, quite a number of the enemy's men had been killed by Naan's bullets, too; there was no anger there – killing the enemy, this was a soldier's everyday activity.

Later, as the years went by, when both wars were

becoming things of the past, Naan thanked God that Abel of Muraka had escaped his bullet then. He recalled his one-time intention with disgust. Naan had realised that if he was told to go to war a third time, he would no longer be able to shoot at a human being. He'd had enough of killing.

Good thing that Abel of Muraka lived; although then there had seemed to be only one way out of that situation.

Abel craved Lilit like mad: ideas like shame and honour were wiped from his head. A bachelor till then, having played around with the village girls – it was said that several children in the neighbourhood looked very much like Abel – he suddenly decided that Lilit must leave Villaku and become his. Day after day Abel roamed around Villaku. His farm hand was managing the farm and he, the farmer, was chasing after another man's wife. Naan doesn't know what Abel said to Lilit, but there were times when his wife came home from milking the cows in the pasture, eyes red from crying.

Abel made no secret that he was trying to persuade Lilit to become his wife. He boasted everywhere that he wouldn't give in, and cursed Johannes, Naan and himself as well. Johannes got blamed for bringing the girl to Villake like a heifer. Stronger words still were used for Naan: such a blockhead should not marry anybody – why blemish the human breed? Abel did not mince his words. Naan should fear God's wrath and not leer at Lilit: he shouldn't put a hand on the woman. So Naan was supposed to be frightened by Abel's cursing.

Abel also insulted himself. What devil had been urging him to chase random women for half his life, wasting valuable time? Long ago he, Abel, should have taken his stick and gone into the world in search of Lilit, before Johannes snatched the girl away and married her to Villaku. That's exactly what he said: married her to Villaku.

Abel wronged Naan by saying that Naan was leering at his own wife. Some time went by before Naan dared to look Lilit in the eye. Nights passed – Naan's heart shivered until he finally ventured to take the woman in his arms.

One night, Lilit and Naan woke up in a fright; coming from the window of their bedroom was a buzzing sound so loud that the whole house was echoing. Naan had jumped up from beside his wife and looked out through the curtains. Staring at the lilacs he'd observed that there wasn't a breath of wind. But the window carried on making a ghastly noise, as if the pane was about to fall out of the frame. It made no sense. It was like someone was drilling into the wood with a giant gimlet, or was it perhaps an earthquake? A tornado would have torn leaves from the trees, smashed the gutters around the roof; that's what makes it clear there has been a tornado.

The buzzing at the window happened almost every night; Naan and Lilit were wasting away from lack of sleep. They worked listlessly in the day, staggering because of exhaustion, and in the evenings they went to their bed worried, not knowing if sleep would come.

They were too embarrassed to talk about their problem in the village, the folk would've had a good laugh: the young couple at Villaku farmhouse have tethered some bogeymen to their window frame.

Finally, Naan told the whole story to Jakob. The owner of Rossa gazed at his nephew for a long while, then shook his head and wondered how Naan could have lived so long without knowing the secret behind such a trivial joke. Jakob explained to Naan at length, as if to a child, how windows are made to buzz. You attach a nail to a thread soaked in pitch, and then stick it into a crack in the the window frame. The perpetrator then stands a little way away and plucks the taut wire like a string.

Naan listened to Jakob, head down, and realised that he was a complete birdbrain. He didn't know the first thing about life.

By the evening Naan had wound himself up; taking the gun from the hook, his anger had become so great that tears were running down his cheeks. He went to the bushes outside the house to wait, and he intended to shoot Abel.

God was protecting Abel, just like he protected Naan as well. Now it gave Naan shivers to even think that he could have been taken away from Villaku in shackles – then he would have lost Lilit forever.

Naan held Lilit's hand tight. A lucky star had followed Naan then.

When Abel saw that Lilit was not giving in, he angrily wooed another woman. He made this decision off the top of his head, took the first girl he met, without bothering to look whether she was standing on straight or crooked legs.

A day before the wedding Abel committed another act of devilry, however. He stole some of Lilit's underwear from the washing line in the yard at Villaku – Roosi happened to see this through the window – filled Lilit's knickers with straw, took the dummy to the top of the land surveyors' tower and pointed the legs towards the sky. The people of Vaseküla had a good laugh for a while. The knickers bleached in the sun there until Joonas climbed up with a boat hook and took the obscenity down.

***

Naan always listened to Lilit. The woman knew how to whisper nicely into his ear so it tickled, making him laugh willy-nilly, and the Master of Villaku never argued with his young wife. All right, one might as well start the autumn ploughing. Jehovah in heaven will also like the sight of the earth turning the yellow straw against its skin for winter. Lilit knew all sorts of old pieces of wisdom, even though she was young: who knows when she had picked those up. And she was determined that Naan must plough the first furrows himself; the soil of the farm wants to see its farmer, otherwise next year's harvest would be lousy – so she believed. Afterwards the farm hand can take over. This is how it usually worked anyway.

And Naan didn't have strength for much more than a couple of furrows. Should Naan plough all of the fields of Villaku in the autumn, the work would last till Christmas.

Naan's body couldn't cope with the toil. He only had to hold the plough for half an hour for it to feel like his shoulder joints were falling apart and his fingers to turn white and numb. His legs stopped obeying him, his shoes shuffled around in the soil of their own accord. Finally, it happened that the horse was pulling the plough, tearing the turf tangled with roots and tugging the master with the plough from one edge of the field to the other. The furrow turned out shallow. Naan used to be told off by Johannes for not treating the field with respect. Naan was not allowed to make a pause in the ploughing then. Johannes appeared immediately, coming out of nowhere, just like he'd been sitting behind the bush and watching his son with a telescope.

With Lilit, life got different, more relaxed. There was no need to worry about the land getting turned inside out; on the second morning Lilit would send the farm hand to the furrow. Lilit didn't bark out orders, didn't watch him with prying eyes – the main thing was to do the first rows, and then Naan could sit down and rest on the bank.

Naan didn't understand why Johannes had battled for Lower Rossa, for Naan and Lilit's children work and bread at Villaku would suffice. Although an old man, he couldn't find peace; Lower Rossa didn't give him his youth back. Johannes had to hire day labourers, he always got slackers or sloppy ones. Not half of his bear's strength was left, but he kept drudging away, let the calves grow, increased the number of cattle. His fingers were already stiff, didn't bend around the cow's teat, but he wanted to get his monthly wad of cash from the office of the dairy co-operative.

A good thing Johannes trusted Lilit and seldom stuck his nose into affairs at Villaku. If Naan still had to listen to Johannes ordering him around, he'd say one day that he was going to war again and that would be that. He would no longer be able to shoot, he would just escape, to say, Africa, to be with the apes. Johannes' rule hadn't brought happiness to anybody. Viida, too, could've run away in her time, when Johannes kept chasing Joakim. Silly her, she didn't let go of the farm and lost her mind all alone, surrounded by her fears.

When they started to recruit men for the Great War, Naan had set off gladly. The further from home he got, the smaller the Ghost Valley shrunk and Villaku seemed completely unimportant – a spot somewhere beside a grove.

But Naan often dreamt of Johannes at night in the war.

Baltic Belles

Father was big, covering the whole sky; instead of a farmer's jacket he was wearing a colonel's uniform and spurs were glimmering on the muddy boots; once he appeared to Naan in a priest's robe, holding a cross in one hand and sprinkling holy water into his son's face with the other. Often, his father was simply standing in the house at Villaku, with something seeming to be glowing in the background. Perhaps Mother didn't want to cower next to Johannes and had her picture hung on the wall for her son to look at. But Naan's eyes weren't very sharp and, moreover, he didn't believe any photographer would have been able to persuade Eeva to go in front of the camera.

When he got back home, he was amazed how accurate his dreams about the wall had been: something was hanging there and indeed it is still hanging there – a sheet of paper with an address written on it in Johannes' hand: Petrograd, Nadezhdinskaya 10. Information about ill and wounded soldiers. Back from the war, hair thinning, Naan experienced paternal love for the first time. Was it affection or just concern about the future of Villaku? Without Naan, Lilit wouldn't have children who belonged in Johannes' family tree.

Naan had very rarely sent letters from the front. He had intentionally kept silent, pretended he couldn't care less about his family. Although he was crouching in some muddy trench stinking of urine, it became increasingly clear to him that life was made up of command and coercion everywhere, and he yearned to get a bullet in himself sooner rather than later. He had willingly sought his death. He didn't hang back in battle and volunteered when braver ones were sought from the ranks. Later, he started to play tricks on Germans by himself. He left his appointed companions in some hollow and crawled in the darkness of night across no man's land to the enemy trench, tied the ends of the ropes he'd brought with him to the wire barrier and crawled back to his trench, letting it out as he went. Sturdy men eagerly grabbed the ends of the line pulled by Naan and dragged the Germans' tangle of wire across the field to their side. Men said Naan was a foolhardy moron. So what: there was no better joke in the war than pulling a barrier from one place to the other! Naan always had a good titter. Sometimes he choked and his whole body shook, having to keep a rag in front of his mouth. Laughing without any noise was like putting spirit up your arse – it makes you drunk but leaves you without full enjoyment.

Later on, dragging wire barriers became Naan's special trick, he offered his services everywhere; the spirals of barbed wire that Naan helped to pull away on the field of battle would have sufficed for the whole county to build cattle fences. Naan's barrier tricks were not for nothing, he wanted to have his fill of laughing before his turn came to get hit by a bullet.

He had thought, let them read the death notice at Villaku and realise that a brave man was killed, because cowards know how to evade a bullet. Unfortunately, the laws of cowardice and bravery didn't hold in real war. It so often happened that shirkers who shoved gold in doctors' pockets, deliberately talked gibberish or made themselves out to be brainy purely to get away from the front line, from the bullets and bayonets. The ones that remained stepped onto mines or got in the way of German shells. War killed people everywhere, its red eye was selecting its victims, finding them also far from the battle field, in places where even the boom of the cannon could not be heard. Vaseküla village had to give its own offering.

Viida's husband got killed by the war between the solid walls of Lower Rossa house, in his own bed. He had wanted to keep away from the trenches and stay at home with his wife. The Tsar hasn't given me any honour or glory, he can send his counts and chamberlains to war, I have nothing but my life and this I'm not giving away – this is what he said, drank a glass of herbal poison and went to the medical committee. Strange disease, the doctors said, scratching their heads, but the man's arms and legs really were trembling and so he got time in hospital. The time passed, and the poison helped again. When Estonian men were ordered to go to an Estonian war, he used his old trick. This time the poison broke him down, seizures came on and they never ended. It's not known whether the drug was accidentally cooked too strong or the man had been weakened by the frequent use of poison. He is said to have suffered tremendously in his last hours. Viida had jumped onto the horse and galloped to the rectory farm to look for the man who had made the drug, but help came too late. When they got to Lower Rossa, Viida's husband had glassy eyes.

The master of Lower Rossa was buried here in the churchyard. But the war still wouldn't leave him alone. The battles had not got anywhere near the village of Vaseküla during either war, but a random bullet hit precisely the cross on Viida's husband's grave and broke its top into splinters.

The war had targeted the master of Lower Rossa and besieged him, until it finally got him at the churchyard, this is what was said in the village of Vaseküla, anyway.

1977

Translated by Eva Finch and Jason Finch

The Seventh Spring of Peace
Viivi Luik

In large grey roadside farmhouses, kulaks had lived and hidden gold inside the legs of iron beds. The mistress of one farm had even hanged herself from a bedpost. A few discarded beds were still lying in the nettles.

A pail was clinking in my mother's hand; we were going to pick rowanberries. Mother wanted to pick a whole pailful of rowanberries and make jam from them for the winter. Even Mann of Orri-Antsu was cooking jam! Everybody was cooking jam! *Every country woman was storing up vitamin-rich rowan jam for the coming winter and improvising out of her old petticoat a new shirt for a five-to-eight-year-old girl!*

Paths were full of water like ditches and grass showed through the clear water, a bubble on every blade and leaf. There were peas growing in the oats in the field, we picked some pods which we gathered in the bottom of the pail, and ate them ravenously all the way. All the way I was begging, "Mother, give us another pod, will you?"

Places became unfamiliar. It seemed to me that we were very far from home and when we'd get back, who knew? We kept having to climb under barbed wire. When we passed someone doing something in their yard, they stopped their work and stared at us. Unfamiliar cows were puffing at us. They may even have been angry bulls. We also saw dogs.

Some of them were like dogs always are – barking loud and wagging their tails at the same time. A person or a cow was always standing somewhere nearby. But others were running around in the scrub, tails between their legs, and squinting at us with the whites of their eyes. It was twilight in the scrub, even during the day. Rain was rustling in the alder leaves, mud sucked the light away; there wasn't grass on the ground, but soil, mud and cow shit.

Low clouds were floating on the alder tops; the rain was not cold, but grey, fine and dense. Earlier, the chickens had been out in the rain and the rooster sang – now it would stay rainy. The forest seemed so thick and strange, as if something was happening there all the time. A narrow path led through thickets. Fungi-covered logs and heaps of rotten twigs were standing beside the path, overgrown with nettles and brambles. A gun or a person could lie buried under them.

Somewhere nearby one said, "Coo-coo-coo-coo," and far away the other one answered, "Coo-coo-coo-coo. I've got six golden eggs, but the crow has five blood-stained brats!"

These were large wild birds, stock doves, and their sad gentle call could be heard from every thicket, as if they were calling back the long-departed summer. As if the two World Wars had never happened, as if there were only strong bicycles, the Jänese goods yard and belief in the new century. Who would've feared a heap of twigs in those days! But I'm still frightened when I see an old pile of brushwood in the forest. What's underneath? The forest, black, sighs, and a shiver runs down the spine, I walk away not looking back, Johannes R. Becher on my mind, "the dark angel leads my steps, the mighty shadow on the cursed century…"

There were good-looking mushrooms growing under the young spruces by the pile of brush. I yelled, "Mother, come here!" and squatted. Suddenly, under the bushy branches, quite hidden, a saucepan came into view. It was enamelled and glossy: we didn't even have one like this. When mother came closer, I said quietly, 'Mother, I found something!'

Mother squatted next to me and tried to look under the spruce with me. She had a white bandana knotted on the back of her head; as ever, she was wearing a print dress, but over it there was a shiny German leather jacket. She wanted nothing but to pick rowan berries, a whole pail of them, and then to make jam from them in the evening. She had been tending cattle and stepped onto a spike. She hadn't been allowed to eat the whole of her pretzel at once, and in the rye she had eaten all the "Kawe" chocolate kept for a rainy day, and got a thrashing for it later. Her godmother had shown her a nice set of maco cotton underwear and promised it to her if my mother could say who the father of Zebedee's sons was. She didn't know and her godmother kept grilling her: 'Who is the mother of your mother's daughters?'

My mother didn't know that either, started bawling and went home, bawling. At home she asked her own mother, "Who is the mother of my mother's daughters?"

Her mother protested, "Do I have to know everything in the world? I don't know!"

Twenty years had passed and now my mother knew very well that it was the Forest Brothers' cooking pot she saw beneath the spruce. She also saw a white notch made with an axe in the trunk of the large spruce, and knew it was a sign. She could guess the names of the Forest Brothers, and she also knew whose sons they were. Now she could've got her maco underwear! But now it would be too small for her, she'd have to give it to me. She was scared of the Forest Brothers; her parents had received land from the new regime. She hadn't seen that cooking pot.

I found it.

I was a big girl now. I could read, I knew what the Bird of Truth was, and the Water of Life; I was well-informed. What were some Forest Brothers in comparison with me? I felt sorry for the enamelled saucepan, I got angry with my mother, threw my legs high up and yelled, 'Nuns and monks, pharaoh! Nuns and monks, pharaoh!' I had read those words in an old school book, connected them to each other and I like them very much. These were mysterious, meaningful words and they sounded particularly ominous screamed out at the top of one's voice. Mother told me to stop but to me it was like water off a duck's back. Mother depended on my grandmother and my uncle, who were her mother and brother. She ate their potatoes and their meat, and she only had twenty-five roubles in money. She was seventeen years older than me and this money she had got from my father. If I wanted to, I yelled. I had dropped onto her lap like a fortune; only from me could she hear:

Teapot, the old chattering mouse,
Goes running off to coffee's house.

Only I could announce to her:

The smoothing iron lets out its breath,
mud puddles awaiting, and death.

And:

Vast and immense is
Moscow with its aerodromes

Baltic Belles

And its gigantic bridges
And the square called Dzerzhinsky,
And the square called Vosstaniya.

I expressed my love by ludicrous trampling, tiresome heavy hanging off her neck and pulling her hair. I cried when she left home, and I made a lot of noise and mucked around when she came back.

No one could stop me when I went to the flowerbed in May, scissors under my apron. I rapaciously cut fat red shoots of peony; I did not spare the bleeding heart, either. The damp earth gave out a sweet smell in the sunshine, it was a joy to cut the juicy flesh of the peony with sharp scissors, and the awareness that a big quarrel, big trouble, was coming squeezed the throat.

Such gifts I made to my mother really quite in passing, just like now with this saucepan.

Mother's round face was sullen and her eyes looked elsewhere. We got to the field. The edges of sky visible here seemed lighter, yellowish. This made me glad and encouraged me.

Ordinary hay seeds had got stuck to our wet legs, but terrible cogged weed seeds had got caught on the hems of our dresses, the same ones that get tangled in dogs' tails in autumn. I picked them off my mother and mother picked them off me.

We followed a mown strip, tall crops were growing on both sides, rain and wind had not beaten it down, this was quite a miracle. But it should have been harvested long ago.

The rowan trees were growing in a row on the same strip. There were six or seven of them. Fine thick trees with low branches, planted by the long-deceased farmer Jaagup of

Tuhka. Holy rowans, truly magical trees.

Seeing them immediately brought an old story to my mind about large trees who move round the world and seek a place of dwelling. They walk on foot and talk to each other. When one stays behind to tie a garter, the others disappear from her sight and she calls, 'Ann and Krööt, ho there! Ann and Krööt, ho there!' and then stays in the place.

I had thought of this or that tree of our neighbourhood that they had arrived on their own accord, but when it came to these rowans, I was certain that Jaagup of Tuhka didn't plant them. They were standing in a full halo against the sky as it cleared, as if they had come from a different land, from Võrumaa or Latvia. Rowan protects a person from the devil. I believed that these ones here certainly did.

I looked at my mother who was cautiously breaking clusters off the branches and throwing them into the bucket. I screwed up my face eating the berries, because they were sour, bitter and juicy. Their flavour contained, and still contains the whole of this landscape, brushwood, stacks of faggots, the sky, the famous autumn rainfalls of the early fifties and my mother's wet glossy leather jacket.

I was standing there, unsuspecting, belly full and red berries in my palm, when the air started to tremble and howl, broke with a jangle, and some jets of water raced over the rowans. They flew in a swarm, they had gulls' wings, they went over so fast that it was like a flash before your eyes. New ones appeared right away, similar ones, with gulls' wings.

I bawled out, "Let's go! Let's go! Let's go! Let's go!"

Not knowing why, I pressed my belly against the ground and felt visible there. There was grass and some big rocks, I squeezed myself between those rocks and yelled in a coarse jerky voice like a sheep or a cow in mortal fear.

Wet post-war Estonia lay all around, the land, crops and trees, rye swaying on the open field, the tall spruce grove murmuring on the hillside.

Mother talked to me, I tried to chase her away. She wouldn't leave, but instead carried on talking about the planes and explained that they won't harm us, that the state won't allow them to harm us. That which flies but utters no birdsong, hums and carries you along.

I crouched under the tree, felt a sharp rock against my thigh and stared at the blue bellflower in the grass. This was a kind familiar creature, it had come here from behind our house so as to give me support. I went to mother and saw that the bucket was almost full of berries. I ordered, "Mother, don't pick any more!" and took her hand. The sky was totally blue, low grey clouds had turned into cumuli with white edges and they were all moving in one direction, towards the distant forest. The light was completely different. The shadow of the forest covered half the field. I looked at the rowans, they were cold red against the sky.

"Let's do a bit of running!" mother said, picked up the bucket, and we hurried along the footpath through the wet rye, in order to get the blood circulating. When the blood circulates, everything is all right. We took a different route back, along the field and across the water meadow. The dried clothes got wet again, water dripped onto you from the rye and the blue of the sky made you shiver. In front of this clear sky all the spruces seemed pitch black. When the shadow of the forest ended, the sun started to warm us and it warmed us so pleasantly and strongly that I had to say, "Mother, let's sit a little!"

Mother took off her jacket and lay it onto a broad flat boulder. We sat in the evening sun, warmed our bones greedily and looked at the distant clouds.

I hadn't been in these places before and didn't even know that they were so close to our home. I sneaked behind my mother and fell onto her unexpectedly like a predatory animal, like a wolf or a lynx. Mother squealed, I made a grr-grr-grr-noise and crawled around her. I shook the buckthorn bush so that black and brown berries fell onto mother. This was a way of driving away the gull-winged planes from my mind's eye. Mother waited patiently, then said, "Well, let's go now," put her jacket back on and took the bucket. The rye field closed behind us like a door and the water meadow began. A couple of kilometres of flat low land, big willows, hay barns, rick bases and cold water, as much as you want. At times water came up to your knee, at times halfway up your thigh. We kept our hems up. A few haystacks were standing on higher spots. Rotten bunches of hay were floating on the water, the surface surrounding the abandoned stacks was rippling. The hay and water smelled sharply cold, as if everything on the earth was withered and bare.

Under the power line, the footbridge went across the river, two thick tarred logs above the black water. The current was fast, the water was burbling quietly and tall dark green reeds were bent towards the current, foam and trash gathering behind them. It gave you a funny sensation walking along these logs, seemingly greasy. Mother took the berry bucket across and then came back to fetch me. She took me on her back, I looked down at the water and believed that right now the white hands of the drowned would come into sight and grab my mother's legs. I had examined such a picture, only there it wasn't a mother with a child who crossed the river but a boy with a square jaw, carrying a large backpack. In the backpack you could see some geese and on the other side of the river the devil was standing, shaking his fist.

No white hands reached out of the water, we got comfortably across the river and in a little while I started to recognise places. I recognised three grey barns that were visible in the distance, and sparse rows of pruned fat-stemmed willows. The water meadow with its retting pools looked like a large river between two distant stripes of forest, broad and clear. Only those thick tall willows and a few ash trees could be seen in the distance like landmarks. Many more trees and bushes were growing on the other side of the river because there were always patches where they didn't make hay there. There were too many hummocks. On that side there were no farms left at all, only the bare water meadows and thick forests.

Under the willow down by the river, Leida of Teiste was soaking the pickling barrel. She raised her red-cheeked face and asked in a harsh voice, "Well where did yer go then, go catching whales, did yer?" She left her work and climbed across slippery stones onto the bank, lowered her voice and asked mother, "Not that yer happened to see the Vahesalu woman, did yer?"

Mother said that we didn't, that we didn't pass the grave. According to Leida, the Vahesalu woman had again started to take flowers to the grave; these had been terribly pretty white flowers, said to be called gladioli.

Leida sighed, "Just think, they left the dead person here in

Baltic Belles

the ground, wouldn't even take him to the churchyard. Won't even let yer put a cross on the ground. Just a wooden statue, with a red star on."

They went silent, gave me funny looks and Leida ordered, "Get on home, child, yer mother will follow you soon." I went as slowly as I could, constantly glancing at Tihase barn; the spruce wood stood bluish behind it – the forest belonged to the state. Mother and I had walked through the other edge of that very forest. It had been so long ago, I didn't believe we'd ever get home, perhaps it wasn't even one day but instead seven years that we'd been away.

I knew very well what grave they were talking about. At Tihase barn one man had been murdered at the time when the collective farms were founded; "a party man", people whispered and looked around. This man was buried in the forest behind the barn, under a birch tree. There had been a raid, but no one was caught, none of the killers. They did find an abandoned bunker and some old sleeves for jumpers, but the new bunker was nowhere to be found. There was a lot of talk about the raid, even time was counted after the raid. I'd been born two years before the raid. The fabric for grandmother's new skirt had been woven during the autumn of the raid.

Now, a couple of weeks ago, a memorial service had been held for the murdered man in the same spruce wood, they made speeches and put wreaths on the grave. But the man's wife had been holding onto a birch with both arms and crying piteously because the cross she had brought was never put on the grave. On every anniversary of the murder she took an armful of flowers into the grove; came from town by bike and left the bike at Teiste; she had to cycle almost sixty kilometres altogether.

Baltic Belles

I didn't know whether the woman was young or old; generally, I didn't grasp what age people were. About someone it was said, "Oh, still a young person, only fifty years old." They talked a lot about this woman, as well as about the bunker. I'd heard those conversations while falling asleep in the evenings, along with the patter of rain outside or the dog's claws on the front-room floor. Sinister forests were roaring around us, full of heaps of twigs and secret paths. The lamp glass broke, at the exact moment the night was at its darkest. Riks of Võtiksaare was spotted in the forest. "Oh the river, the broad Ural! No light, no single sound!" I boomed to grandmother for encouragement when she, holding a lantern, went to the cowshed in the evening, to tend the animals.

The Vahesalu grave was something that should not have been there. It gave a sinister appearance to the seats made from riverside rushes and forget-me-nots picked from the water meadow, and the marsh air could flicker in the heat of a summer's day as it liked, Tihase barn and the dark spruce grove were still visible through it.

My shadow, usually so short, had now grown long and black. I was walking alone along the path towards home. I stopped by the bushes at the edge of the water meadow and looked back at the clearing I had walked through. It was surrounded by distant forest on all sides and covered by sky above. My thighs were cold, my arms covered in goosebumps. I saw flat land with occasional round shrubs, cursed and abandoned and hard-won land. Swallows were rushing now high to the sky, now low near the ground. They were black and the sky behind them seemed vast and eternal. The water meadow and the sky together looked like a glass picture. In the nettles and alders framing this magical perspective rusty barbed wire and lopsided fence posts could be found. Barbed wire was everywhere. You had to step cautiously, clenching your toes, because former cattle fences and village streets, and the sunken borders of farmlands were lurking for the soles of your feet in the tall grass. Wire was also rusting around the trenches, threatening blood poisoning, pain and suffering.

I still saw mother standing by the river, she looked straight and flat like a figure cut out of paper. Occasionally she nodded her head.

I turned around and quietly started to walk along the edge of the Teiste potato field. On the left there was a thick copse of damson bushes, behind which a house stood, surrounded by big trees. There was a path through the bushes, from which you could see the upstairs window. In the sun it always shone greenish blue, as if oily. You had to walk quietly here, so the dogs wouldn't hear you. Straight ahead, the tall spruces of Vanatare were in sight. You had to cross the cart road, now the long grey cowshed and stables were on your right, both empty, the manure still there, doors wide open, the low frame of a boarded-up watering point for cattle. On the left, through lilacs and jasmines you could see a dwelling house. It had been built on the site of the old farm house, old garden trees and decorative bushes surrounded it, the stone of the front steps read '1939', the copper door handles were glossy, the proud perennial flowerbeds were not yet completely overgrown, there were white phloxes and colourful Sweet Williams, but someone had secretly dug up the poppies and taken them God knows where. The millstone table was still waiting in the lilac gazebo, benches in a semicircle around it. In the yard, in the centre of a round patch of daisies, an empty flagpole was towering; the gold-coloured tip of the lightning rod was glistening on the roof. The house stood there like a coffin, tall, brown, with glossy handles.

I climbed onto the stones of the basement and grabbed the window ledge. As always, I saw the floor of the living room, the same covers of *Taluperenaine*, the farmer's wife magazine still lying there. The evening sun shone in through the door, as the door between two rooms was open. Here everything seemed as it should be to me; nothing had changed.

Now I went round the corner and took a concerned owner's look at Ärna's old room. The same dried butterfly was still between the windows and white satin shoes with buttons were lying on the floor. On the wall of Ärna's old room I could see the clock, it could strike any moment. The clock was ticking. Every other day Juuli – mother of August of Vanatare, grandmother of the Forest Brothers – came here and wound the clock up. The clock was not allowed to stop. When the clock stopped, August would die in the cold land. Now everything depended on the clock, its wheels, its weights, its pendulum and its chain. The clock could kill August, but it could also take mercy on him and leave him alive. August's mother was not allowed to go into the house; everything had been taken away from there and the doors locked. But Juuli wanted to pull up the weights and thus save August's life, therefore she carried the door key on a string under her jacket and always carefully glanced to each side when unlocking the door. She was afraid of the chairman of the village council. She wasn't afraid of me, although I watched unashamed when she said the Lord's Prayer under the clock. Once she even gave me a piece of light blue pre-war soap. Another time I myself found a thin grey picture book under the cupboard, *Hitler: Children's Friend*.

I then looked at the pictures in the lilac gazebo, waiting for August's mother to leave so as to take a good look round myself. Actually, I was waiting for her to die, but I didn't want her to die here, then I would've got frightened, first of all I wouldn't even have dared come to the house. I kept turning the pages of the book found under the cupboard and saw in the pictures little girls in white dresses in the *Führer*'s country house. Snowy mountain tops could be seen through the big windows, vases were full of flowers, the furniture was smooth and beautiful. The little girls' faces were half shy and half vain, they were licking big porridge spoons or pushing a doll's pram to and fro on the lawn. Occasionally they had to experience the touch and smell of Hitler's jacket and moustache, and the warmth of his body, when he bent over them or squatted before them and held their hands in his. Bigger girls with blond plaits and full skirts brought him armfuls of German field flowers. Little boys were standing in a line singing, their eyes were shining, short curls were flowing, they were wearing strong boots and ribbed knee socks. In the park, under a big tree the Leader himself was standing; he was standing in a silly way, as if peeing into the bush.

When August's mother finally left, I hid the book between the foundations and the wall of the house. I wanted to look at these pictures again, but not at home, where uncle would say, "Well why should such things be given to the child?" and look at mother.

I wanted to open the window of Ärna's old room and

climb in. I knew that this window was easy to open but difficult to close. I stood on the ledge of the stone foundations for a long while, unable to decide. I had seen with my own eyes that August's mother took the blue soap from under the floorboards in the anteroom. What else could be there, I didn't know, I would have wanted to lift the floorboard myself and look. Perhaps there were some picture books, or perhaps sugar? Or knives with plexiglass handles? Or silver paper? I was too small, I couldn't very easily climb in the window and I was, in fact, scared, too. What if I couldn't get out and had to stay in there? The sun would roll down, the floor creak and the clock strike. August's sons Harald and Heldur will come from the forest at night, singing:

"I left you for good.
Now in faraway lands
Cruel fate treats me only
With torturing hands.
And
Just say the little word 'adieu'
If you must go away from me..."

As they sing, they take from me their soap, their book, their sugar, their knives and their silver paper and then grab my throat, while Riks of Võtiksaare looks on with his white eyes, beating the rhythm with his foot.

The grass in the garden is tall and wet, the book in the crack in the foundations could be quite soaked by now. The blackcurrant leaves and phloxes let off a strong smell, the wind and rain had beaten down the flowers, the white clusters of blossom were visible though the grass like human faces. If I wanted to, I could break them off and throw them away. I could throw them through the windows, I could gobble gooseberries in other people's gardens in broad daylight. I had eaten most of the berries unripe, but those that managed to ripen, tasted particularly sweet, large, yellow and soft. The apples weren't ripe yet, because here there were only winter sorts: Livonian Onion, Golding and the sharp red one that used to be referred to as 'sodding Alexander'. I could bend the branches of the apple trees until they broke with a crack, I could bite into the apples still on the trees and then spit the pieces out, I could climb into the old short-stemmed cherry trees and break their tops, if I couldn't get the fruit otherwise. Inside me the owner was fighting with the destroyer. I wanted everything to be in good order, I got annoyed when I saw an unfamiliar cow chained up in the berry patch or when the Teiste ram was chewing the blackcurrant branches. I had already seen two gardens like this; both I considered mine.

But there were four farms in the neighbourhood which I made a note of. I fervently hoped that the people of these farms would be taken away somewhere too. On one farm an apple pear and a Suislepp apple tree grew with exceptionally big and juicy apples; on the other, the river was right next to the yard and there was a boat standing by the river. I wanted to row the boat myself and bathe in the other farm's sandy bathing place myself. There were so many strawberries behind the third farm that the ground was red from them, but it wouldn't do to pick them under those people's windows when they were still in there.

In the fourth farm there was a bookcase with glass doors

full of books. In the drawers there were old German fashion magazines. I wanted to look at the books, also those that weren't otherwise given to me; from the fashion magazines I intended to cut out the prettiest women and play with them behind the woodpile.

Toil and struggle were ridiculous words, the invention of stolid farmers. What toil and struggle was there for me? Look, I had as many flowerbeds, trees, bushes and berries as I wanted.

Squinting my eyes I saw the face of the clock through the dusty windowpane, a dull-coloured picture of a landscape above and black hands below, inside the circle of numbers. The pendulum moved solemnly back and forth and, through the lilac bushes, greenish yellow anguish poured over the two limp satin shoes.

Then I heard the creak of the bucket handle, my mother's head was moving behind the shrubs. I called, "Mother, where are you going, I'll come too!" and climbed off the ledge above the basement. You had to step cautiously here because all sorts of trash could be found on the ground: broken jars and bottles, boards with rusty nails in, bits of hayfork and old iron rakes.

Mother was surprised. "I thought you'd gone home!"

And I answered hypocritically, "But I was waiting for you!"

The sky was red and the sun started to go down. Smoke went straight up from our chimney, the door was wide open and grandmother, wearing a hemp apron and a calico jacket with patched elbows, was in the shed, chopping grass for the pig. Eighteen years remained until her death.

She had only been to Viljandi, Tarvastu, Põltsamaa and

Kolga-Jaani. No one had taught her German. In Russian she knew six words. These were *odin, tva, kuritsa, petuhh, russki tsaar* and *idii sjudaa*, which she pronounced *idissu taa*.

She had given the collective farm two cows, an in-calf heifer and an old black gelding. I tried to turn her around, I threw a broomstick at her, I loved her.

Chickens had crapped in the porch and grandmother was admonishing: "You bloody souls of the body! I'll give you what for!"

When she saw us, she complained, "Drags this child along all the time. It's already evening but you just can't find your way back home."

Her harsh voice, big face and grey hair reminded me of somebody in the Bible stories, who hits the rock with a stick and, see, water bursts out of the rock. Old white clouds are moving above and the wind is moving the hems of the people's Jewish robes. The distant future of mankind has bad surprises in store for them, which will later be described as follows: "At one time, gas chambers could kill up to eight thousand people. Every crematorium burnt three corpses in twenty minutes. The corpses were burnt in such numbers that flames rose from the chimneys. The chimneys cracked from the heat so they had to be reinforced with iron hoops."

I coloured those old earnest Bible pictures with "Spartacus" coloured pencils, but something always remained visible. I made long reddish-brown cloaks for semi-clad men; the angels' wings I turned into aeroplane wings.

Grandmother had potato soup cooking, mother started to potter around with the rowan berries, she took one scoop of hot water after another from the back cauldron and poured them onto the berries, this was supposed to make them softer.

Again I saw things that were *ours*. They were in the front room and in the back, in the porch, kitchen and the larder. Two wooden beds were still standing in the back chamber, as if I hadn't been away for a long time. Also a dark brown wardrobe and two tables – one of them large and white, with thick legs, the other small and brown, with thin legs and a fringed table cloth. Above grandmother's bed hung, just as it had done for my whole lifetime, my dead aunt's large mirror. The walls were covered in hooks and nails – black, dark blue or sheep-brown clothes; coats and jackets were hanging on all of the hooks and nails.

From the end window the low evening sun shone onto the edge of the mirror and this made a rainbow on the wall. Blue, red, green, yellow and orange were showing off proudly. This was a beautiful light, a summary of all these red stripes of the evening that I was to see in the future or those that in the evenings of the world had been looked at before me.

"The sun, legendary red, blazing through far-off hazes of smouldering woods, sets before my hurting, feverish eyes..." Gustav Suits once wrote.[1] Was this *that*? At any rate, this light said clearly and proudly, both in our back chamber and in other rooms and other decades, that time is moving.

Colours moved across the wall like a procession of fairies; on the door cornice grey home-cooked soaps were standing in a row; in the wardrobe a large white sugar sack was rearing up like a polar bear. Sugar is difficult to come by, so sugar has to be looked after! The sugar sack was crazy about me, it wanted me to feel if it was still intact and check whether perhaps the

---
[1] English translation by Ants Oras.

top had been left untied. Day after day I fought the sugar sack.

Mother came into the backroom, the wardrobe door squeaked, the sugar sack was indeed taken out. Mother measured sugar with the one-litre tin mug. I licked my lips and quickly stuck them into the yellowish heap of sugar. I gulped the sugar, cold came in through the open doors, the cow's chain clinked in the cow barn, in the front room *Heidi* was lying on the dining table, its sheets as yellow as this damp and clumpy sugar in front of my face. Weaver's reeds could be seen between the beams. The beams themselves were square, thick and brown. The whole ceiling was brown.

I followed mother to the kitchen. It wasn't dark outside, but the lantern had already been lit in the kitchen. Grandmother was crushing the boiled potatoes with her hand into the pig food, steam was rising from the cauldrons and the walls were sweating. For fifty years grandmother had crushed potatoes for the pigs here. This high narrow room with its sooty ceiling, a wooden peel and the stove broom in the corner behind the door, pig-sticking knives on the walls. The bench for the water bucket, the chopping block and wash basin. Lace-trimmed paper on the shelves, which held rusty old confectionery tins containing caraway seeds, peppermint stems and lime blossoms. A window with two panes and a cold cement floor.

Dishwashers, *fridges*, light blue tiling and white *tiling*, *plastic* table tops, *stick-legged* stools, *toasted* bread, *orange juice*, soft-boiled breakfast eggs were only a few hundred kilometres away, terrifying and unimaginable. Somewhere lived people who skinned their herring before starting to eat it. They can't deal with the skin and bones, well, well! Somewhere water was already running into the bath, it was

Baltic Belles

children's bedtime, mirrors got steamy, thick bath towels were hanging on the hooks waiting, beds had been made, nightdresses were put on the children. The nightdress was not Juhan the shopkeeper's daughter's old red dress that is put on you for the night instead of a nightdress, but something completely different. Everyone knows what a nightdress is.

Perhaps children were bathed at the time also in Sarkanarmijas iela and Vabaduse puiestee, but this was certainly happening in Lönnrotinkatu and Valhallavägen. The same cold redness above hundreds of thousands of houses, darkening green, on an August evening in 1950.

My mother poured sugar into the pot and stirred the berries with a wooden spoon that had been worn flat. Grandmother came in and said, "The fog is so cold tonight, I wonder if it'll bite the potato stalks?"

I took the soup plates and spoons into the front room. Grandmother pulled the front-room curtains and turned the light on. Usually the light was not lit in summer ("Whoever turns the light on in summer, stops the grass growing under their window!") but now it was dark and we were eating late. Grandmother brought the soup bowl, the herring plate, half a loaf of bread, knives and spoons onto the table. The dog uttered a bark outside, uncle was coming home, I ran thudding to the porch. It smelled weird there.

"What smell is that?" Uncle asked and opened the door wide.

Grandmother put her hands on her belly under the apron and gloated, "Well she's mucking around with her jam again! The house is full of the smell of burning!"

This was a great blow for me. That means, mother's jam

burnt, and *the sugar went to waste*. The lantern was hanging on the flue hook, a sad yellow light was cast into the pot, which Mother was scraping with the spoon. We were standing at the door, me, Uncle and Grandmother. Everybody was silent. A fat moth was flying around the lantern.

How far were those rowans now, how empty could the water meadow be! Where did sugar come from, anyway? Was it pre-war sugar? What sugar was this? Oh, the world was collapsing, and there will be no jam, this good thick jam, this is all mother's fault.

"Mother, this is all your fault!" I said angrily. "Mother, don't you see that you're to blame!" I went to the range and pushed mother with all my might. This meant: "Mother, you're to blame that I've got a skeleton, blood, organs and flesh!" "Mother, you're to blame that I'm scared of planes!"

The others had gone into the front room and were slurping down the soup. The dog was probably given a bone because it was chewing on something cracking for a long time. Mother sat down on the block and started to cry. Her back was all round and she was swaying forward and back wilfully. I hadn't ever seen her cry much. Her mouth was crooked and her face was red. The spoon fell into the ashes and stayed there. Grandmother called from the other room, "Come and eat now! What are you doing there?"

Uncle grumbled, "What are you hassling them for all the time? Don't they know themselves that the food is on the table?"

Mother wept, "Oh god, oh my god... four kilos of sugar..." The light was flickering and the moth was buzzing around the lantern, the kitchen was almost dark.

Baltic Belles

I wanted to eat, I wanted a slice of bread and some thick potato and barley soup. I felt very sorry for myself but I couldn't leave the kitchen. I had to stay and watch. Something more might happen. Perhaps mother would get some more sugar now and burn that, too, if I don't stop her. Perhaps a blue flame will come up from the pot all of a sudden and a grey old man will appear, who wants to know mother's greatest wish. Mother wishes for four kilos of sugar and all is well again.

Mother's shadow was hovering on the ceiling, nothing happened, I pestered her, "Mother, come on, let's eat!"

Mother blew her nose into her headscarf but wouldn't stand up. She said snappily, "Well, stop bothering me. Go yourself if you want!"

Tommi was sleeping under the dining table, the soup was cooling down but still hot. Grandmother pressed the loaf of bread against her chest and cut me a medium-thick slice, pushed it towards me and said, "There, have this!"

Grandmother always sat at the end of the table, she cut the crust off the bread because she had no teeth. She'd had enough toil and now she wanted to eat in peace. She had planted lilies of the valley and ferns on the site of her grave, next to Grandfather's.

Perhaps she anticipated that a grand dark red sunset would shine through the big trees of the Riga Road graveyard in Viljandi in August 1978, that it would glint back from the brick wall surrounding the old landlord's graves, and also shine back from the low whitewashed chapel. Does Grandmother foresee that in the cream jar at our feet there are humble yellow flowers, that the brown wooden cross placed there for her is already decaying. Mother in her newly done curls politely asks, "Will you now remember where Grandmother's grave is?" Muttering comes from the distant overgrown corners of the graveyard, bums and drunks are already there. Nobody now warns me against the end of the world: I can lie, cut pictures out of books, use a totally intact pillowcase for a rag, throw away food, deceive a friend, beat a dumb animal with a cane, sneer at someone else, hand over a stone in place of bread.

Grandmother was sucking bone marrow, she had broad hands and the headscarf pointed up above her forehead. Her face looked out of the headscarf as if from an arched church window. Behind her the years 1900 to 1910 were hovering. Then she also had had a white blouse, two brown velvet ribbons on the hem of her skirt and a bouffant hairstyle.

There were three vertical lines above the bridge of her nose, it took her a long time to chew her piece of bread. I'd seen her cursing, swearing and cracking a joke. Now she and Uncle were talking about collective farm stuff, occasionally grandmother got angry and her face flushed, then she banged the knife handle against the table: "You bloody souls of the body! You'll see starvation, you will!"

That might have been about the cattle women who threw calf corpses into the ditch, or about crops that were allowed to rot in the fields. Or perhaps hay had heated up in the haystack. All possible.

Uncle cut some lard onto his bread; he was a stocky man with a red face, bright white teeth and a greying moustache. The top of his head was shiny, his hair had fallen out in the war. He usually wore a grey high-peaked cap. Sometimes people said, "Hans went to Latiku to slaughter the pig," or "Hans is at Pajusi slaughtering the calf." Then Uncle would be wearing old blood-stained clothes when he came home, carrying under his arm a piece of fresh meat wrapped in newspaper.

In this room, on the wall above the end of the workbench was his cupboard. He had made the cupboard himself before the war, it was dark brown. In this cupboard there was some leather for boots, awls, pitch and waxed end, a block of light blue shaving stone, some studs, nails, a home-made knife with an acrylic glass handle. The handle was transparent with red stripes. It made you want to lick it because it resembled a caramel. And boot lasts that looked like yellow and bony human feet. Those lasts made the cupboard quite unpleasant to me. On the top shelf there was a hair clipper that you could shave heads with. It was shiny, it had two handles like an animal's paws. But the razors had ivory handles. When they weren't used for shaving, the thin blade stayed hidden inside the handle. Uncle was good at sharpening razors. Also at sharpening scythes, axes and saws. Knives always tried to cut my finger, saws came crashing down onto me. But my Uncle raised the razor to his throat and the blade obeyed him, it didn't cut his veins. Razors were honed, axes were sharpened on the grindstone, the teeth of the saw were bent and the scythe was whetted. The whet was also in Uncle's cupboard. In the front there were pipes. Two short stumpy pipes, copper rings around the stem. The smell of pipe came out of them and they were dark inside, there were Uncle's toothmarks on their stems. These were the pipes of a farm hand.

Uncle's grandfather had been a corvée labourer. Uncle himself was a skilled cartmaker and saving money when he was as young as twenty. When he came home after the war years, ridden with lice, his feet swollen in his boots, he found me.

Baltic Belles

Uncle's pipes were humble and fierce. When you turn your back, they will jump at you and bite into your calf.

I gobbled the soup and shook my legs under the table. The more I enjoyed the food, the more wildly my legs moved.

But it was rarely enjoyable. Whether the cow was dry and you had to eat pearl barley cooked with water, or the meat ran out before spring, or the potatoes had to be kept for seed. But sometimes, when the pig had been slaughtered, there was a feast – a big bowl of fatty pork with turnip was cooked. I didn't eat that, I sulked on my own. Then grandmother marvelled, "What on earth might the child want then when even this good food won't do?"

I bawled, "Human flesh!" and laughed loudly. With *one* word I could turn other people's faces angry or shocked, with one word I could cause a big row.

Dopey flies were buzzing at the ceiling, mother was clanking things in the kitchen, I was sleepy, full and tired, but I still looked round carefully in the room to spot something that might scare me before the night. The door of the brown cupboard was closed, the pipes weren't visible. Everything was all right with the backroom, there was nothing particularly horrible there. Below the front room coat rack Uncle's patent leather tall boots were standing; they were a bit dubious.

Suddenly my spoon halted, I turned all stiff, sat like a post and the corners of my mouth turned downwards. On the work bench there was sitting my doll Mann, whom I feared in the evenings. This Mann was ancient, at least fifty years of age if not older. She had on her a dark blue woolly dress with a pink front, but this dress was much newer and wasn't hers. Although the dress was too large for her, it still looked like a baby dress on an old hag. Mann's body under the dress was covered in soiled black and grey striped cloth, her arms and thighs were limp, there was nothing inside them, but in the body they said there was seaweed. The hands, feet and head were of stone.

In fact, this "stone" meant that you could bang Mann's head against anything, even against the stove, and she never split. She tempted you to yell, "Slam the legs and head against the wall." Fifty years running the farm girls had been doing exactly this to her, but she had still survived and got to me, with her stone hair (these were supposed to be hazel curls), her one brown eye, because the other eye had long since disappeared. The nose no longer existed and in the place of chubby pink art nouveau cheeks one could see chipped grey matter. She might've had head lice, she might've begged or shuffled in the bins or got drunk. This was perhaps an old filthy hag, not a child's toy.

Actually, a picture of an old hag resembling Mann was in a German language book in the table drawer in the backroom. In the picture, a dead body in a wide dress was walking, a scythe over her shoulder, but you weren't allowed to look at this picture or even touch the book. It belonged to the school headmaster, who had been taken away, and grandmother was looking after it. When the headmaster eventually comes back from afar, a surprise will be awaiting him in his home country, something from his home, even if it's just a book with a picture of death in it.

I said, "Again this Mann is here! Grandmother, take Mann to the larder."

Grandmother's knees were cracking when she got up

from the table. Without a word she went to the work bench, stuck Mann under her arm, picked up the plates from the table and chased the dog out.

Mother had got the pot clean and was drying the kitchen floor. Her eyes seemed grey and her face wasn't moving. She was blaming the pot and the range for burning the sugar.

Grandmother urged me, "You go to bed now."

Mother poured some tepid water out and put the basin in front of the range. I sat on the chopping block and stuck my feet into the basin, paddled a bit and demanded, "Gimme a towel! Gimme a towel!"

Mother brought the grey housekeeping soap and started to scrub my feet with it, then she dried them with the old floral apron which served as a towel. When I finally got up to go, I immediately went to the backroom, to bed. The hay was rustling in the bed sack, as it had just been stuffed. In the place of a nightdress I had to put on an old dress, things were used in the place of other things all the time. An apron in the place of a towel, a dress in the place of a nightie, galoshes in the place of shoes, Mann in the place of a doll.

Uncle's bed was creaking, he was going to bed; Grandmother came in and hooked the door. A bright moon was shining in later that night. A white thing was hovering in the corner of the stove; that was my mother's headscarf hanging off the damper of the stove. My legs were twitching and I kicked them under the thin red blanket. My bones were growing; my body was getting bigger and bigger.

1985

Translated by Eva Finch and Jason Finch

Ella
Elin Toona

Ella's "Peipus grey" eyes (that's how they remembered her in the lakeside village of Kodavere) found something new and intriguing in every day. She would quickly grab a pencil and a scrap of paper, sometimes bloodstained butcher's paper taken from a slab of meat, because time was of the essence, then sit on the edge of the bed and, with a couple of strokes, rapidly sketch the moment of inspiration that had struck her in the kitchen. She had recorded Liki and Elin on paper both in peacetime and in wartime, in good times and bad, and had observed how the traces of time were all identical in the end, though never the kind that could be guessed or imagined. The surroundings changed, but faces always held the same faith and hope. She saw it in the guests who sat on her daughter Liki's bed and told their news in detail and at length, or in her granddaughter Elin's English girlfriends who had already grown accustomed to the "foreigners'" one-room dwelling and asked Liki to lay their tarot cards. They needed to know: Does he love me? Will I be famous? In one drawing, Liki is sitting at the desk and laying cards, a cigarette hanging from the corner of her mouth. How nice it was to dream about the future when it was yet unknown!

Ella observed from the side, marvelling at how quickly her own future had arrived. She could never have imagined

Baltic Belles

that she would one day live a quiet and peaceful life in London, in a warm apartment, cooking in her own kitchen once more. Sometimes, when sitting serenely in her rocking chair and thinking back upon the past, life seemed like a fairytale – "*Ein Märchen aus uralten Zeiten*"[2] as Erni would have said, quoting Heine. The war years were over, Estonia was a distant memory, and the Americans had already walked on the Moon, but Estonians still couldn't return to their homeland. The latter fact was the greatest mystery and injustice of her whole life; however, she had come to decide that her personal happiness was no longer somewhere in the distant future, but right here in her one-room London apartment. Liki was retired. Elin had returned from Singapore, had travelled the world, re-married, and now lived in America. She had an American husband and a tiny son named Timothy-Rein. Elin had been Ella's greatest worry, but now that the girl had a husband and child, there was no need to fear she'd be left alone. The future was the dream of the young. It was a fantasy, the introduction and chapter one of all fairytales.

I didn't know Ella, I only knew Mämmä. Grandma was always "old" in my eyes but stayed the same, because she was already old when I was born. It felt like I alone was the one who changed. Mother Liki's changes took place outside our consciousness. She was always "there" but not with us, and that's why I chose the London apartment where the three of us were finally together again as the introduction to "Ella". Ella, my grandmother, was our home, our past, and our future. Everything outside of her had been nasty, strange, rented, temporary, and ephemeral for a long time, and now, that final

---

2 A fairytale from ancient times (German).

home, past, and certainty also had to come to an end.

One's life story, in the modern sense, is akin to a film playing in two dimensions. The first rolls nights and days in the background, in memory and thoughts, while the second continually records new impressions and experiences. Every film's wheels are oiled by a leitmotif that is already familiar or was established long ago – one that echoes in your ears and provides intellectual fluency.

Grandma always heard and saw much farther than I did. When I was little and we sat on Tchaikovsky's bench on Haapsalu's seaside promenade and her eyes came to rest on the emptiness of the heavens, I quickly pressed my cheek against hers to see what she saw. I also pressed my ear against hers to hear what she heard. Still, I never heard anything but her breathing, and saw only clouds and water. I hadn't gone out into the world yet and had only heard music at home, but I also wanted to see the things she called "life" and "memory", because she had lived there without me and I was jealous of everything where I wasn't.

"You'll certainly see life when you grow up," was her reassuring response.

"Will I get memories then, too?" I asked.

"They'll come of their own accord. They are what life is made up of."

I couldn't understand that then, and must admit that I came to understand many things Grandma attempted to tell me over the years far too late. Such as, for instance, how the existence of a person's entire life, a family, and even a nation can expire if you can't tell someone about them in the same language of that land!

Baltic Belles

For a week, I sat constantly at her side in London, chatting. We were together just as we'd always been, but both of us knew it would be as our last time in this world. I still spoke Estonian thanks to her, although it was no longer my language at home and each forgotten word shuttered a window into my own past.

Grandma sat in the rocking chair and I beside her, but I felt like I was blabbering away too much – as if I was at the cinema and interrupting the progression of the story for those who listened better and had a better understanding of things. I heard myself repeating things I'd said long ago, things we'd discussed long ago. We would always watch the last candle burn down on the Christmas tree on Christmas Eve in the very same way: a time, when we felt a need to be silent and to wrap ourselves up in it; to pull peace and a natural ending – not panic – around us.

Mum had said on the phone: "Come visit if you can. Mämmä isn't the same any more. You'll have the chance to talk a little still." I came as quickly as I could. My husband was sick, our son was in school. I couldn't stay for long, even though I'd already sensed the invitation in Mämmä's last letter, which was nearly illegible. It had arrived like a mysterious papyrus scroll covered in hieroglyphics, with thoughts plucked from all across time and eternity, through which I managed to pick out the words: "Long live beauty and goodness!"

Mum was right: Grandma wasn't "the same" any more. The break-in at our apartment in the fall of 1970 had left her with deep wounds. She recovered from the physical wounds, but the experience shocked her so profoundly that her inner flame began to flicker out, and in the spring of 1974, it was clear that the sparks of life were fleeing her mortal frame and already

Baltic Belles

illuminating new lands. Although we sat side by side, her eyes constantly drifted past me, over the rooftops, up towards the greyish-white heavens, farther than my gaze could reach. We had come to a fork in the path and could no longer continue the journey together. I considered pressing my cheek against hers again, but in the intervening years I'd already studied her life and listened to her music, and the saddest thing of all was knowing that everything we'd spoken about, everything we'd lived through together and carried along with us had to be left behind here, on Finborough Road. Here was the end of our long journey together. Her things were to stay at Mum's at first, but for how long? Mum didn't want to move to America. The greatest loss was mine to bear. For as long as Mum and Grandma were alive, I had a spiritual home, homeland, and memories. To be in a world without memories where you were unable to translate your thoughts or share your visions with others, not even with your own children, must have been the most dreadful kind of loneliness there is. That is what I feared the very most: I wanted to cling to memories like a child grasping for a ray of sunshine.

Mum sat on a stool by the window and smoked. Grandma was in the rocking chair, her old slippers on her feet and a knitted scarf draped over her shoulders. It was cold inside. The central heating was acting up because the building owner wanted to get rid of the old tenants. In the surge of Thatcherite privatisation, everyone had the opportunity to become a house or apartment owner. Central London was prime real estate. Flats could be scooped up for next to nothing, renovated into upmarket rental properties, and then resold at a massive profit. The Chelsea-Kensington neighbourhood was especially cheap.

Since elderly residents couldn't simply be tossed out onto the street, especially with rents still under state control, landlords tried to harry them with cold water and tepid radiators until they left of their own accord. The cosy London life they had enjoyed was coming to another end, though Mum reckoned that if they really did have to move, they'd be given a nice retirement apartment in a London suburb where many of her friends already lived. She often said, "You see, England wasn't such a bad choice after all!" astonishing even herself with words that would never have crossed her lips before! Grandma was likewise amazed every time a social worker came to cut her toenails and she was asked whether she really didn't need anything. And she was utterly bewildered when she was given £10 at Christmastime – "for buying presents".

"Just imagine: in this country, you're paid for being old!"

We'd been away from Estonia for thirty long, long years. Some of them, like a dreamless night, were spent in a dark room, until we finally reached a new dawn – although it was one in a strange world. We got by, but we maintained our hope that Estonia would one day be free.

I hadn't forgotten anything. I had remained Estonian but didn't know that a person loses herself if she cannot describe her memories to others, cannot read relatives' letters aloud, cannot convey her favourite poem or books, because they are in another language and lose their cultural merit even in the best translation. Part of me had allowed myself to be moulded and channelled like rain trickling down a windowpane. I hadn't forgotten anything, but what good is a memory that lacks familiar sounds? We only know what we know! Everything else has to be read between the lines. And such is the case of

Baltic Belles

Ella's life story: the refugee history of three generations, the final story of an individual!

2008

Translated by Adam Cullen

Lying Tiger
Lilli Promet
(Eduard Wiiralt. Vernis-mou.)

The great graphic artist Eduard Wiiralt was absorbed in his work, his expression, which was otherwise so solemn and guarded, displaying a gentle mildness. He appeared to be entranced by good ideas.

The tiger, on the other hand, felt tetchy. He kept his tail still and close to his leg, didn't flick it around, stared straight at the master with a languid gaze, and was in a comfortable position. But his sense of well-being was merely superficial. In truth, he was restless because something alien was unfolding around him; something unfamiliar that nagged at him.

"Hey, say there: you do realise what strange trees you've planted around me?" the tiger asked.

"Naturally. They're birches," the master replied without glancing up from his work.

"Why did you plant birches around me when I'm not familiar with them?"

"So that I would feel the proximity of my homeland," the great artist said.

"I'm excited by these birches of yours," the tiger said.

"You know, tiger – I am, too," the man acknowledged.

The tiger knew very well that the great artist didn't want to speak any more, but he just felt so incredibly uncomfortable among the strange, foreign trees, and so, he simply couldn't hold himself back.

"I know grasslands, savannas, and valleys. I know dry and fiery wind, and long rainfalls that make the flamingos cry.

"I know blossoming grasses, deep-watered rivers, and the musk of tangled forests.

"I've seen mountains and have observed ibises above me.

"I know baobabs as high as the sun, wild fig trees, mango trees with their limbs stretched wide, and lianas dangling in knots and nooses above me, filled with screeching apes.

"I know – Oho! – unimaginable forest clearings, stomping grounds and mating sites, and many a good watering hole and hiding place, but I do not know your birches.

"And if I'm lying, then may I turn into a worthless runt of a jackal this instant!"

"You're not lying, tiger. Neither have you exaggerated or embellished your knowledge," the great artist said. "But in addition to the trees he knows, every man furthermore has dream trees that others do not, and truly cannot, know."

"Then tell me at least: what are these birches of yours like, and what you might compare them to?"

"There's nothing they can be compared to, tiger. They sprout in my heart, their roots are in my soul, and their crowns are in my imagination," the great artist spoke with the same mild melancholy that hadn't lifted the whole time he'd been working.

The tiger was amazed that the man was speaking so much: ordinarily, he could only get a word or two out of him, and that was like pulling teeth. Once, one of the president's ministers paid him a visit in Paris, where they sat in their chairs for two hours and, over the course of that whole time, the great artist himself spoke only two words: "Hello" at the beginning and "Goodbye" at the end. The guest himself carried the rest of the conversation.

But now, the great artist intended to speak, so the tiger crossed his paws and settled in to listen.

"These birches that grow in my homeland," the man spoke, "they are the prototypes for my imaginary birches. I can certainly tell you about them. Would you like that?"

"Be my guest," encouraged the tiger, who had a mere jungle upbringing and was completely uneducated.

The master held his head between his hands, thought for a few moments, and then this is what he said:

"How wonderful it is to daydream beneath a birch tree.

"You lie down on your side in the grass and watch the clouds or the buttercups' yellow faces blossoming around you. The sun despises the snow in springtime and when the final crusts of ice melt, the forest's juices start flowing. And the white birch in front of the shed door, as old as an ancient serf of this world, unsheathes its leaves.

"You, tiger, have not heard the way rain patters in a birch grove. The smell of damp birch trees is the smell of my childhood, and the black as night starling my cheerful childhood songbird. But a little switch of birch shoots has always ensured the body is trained and the soul is not led to ruin. For it is the hide-tanners, and they alone, who know why it is fair and necessary.

"I'm joking, tiger. You should never take everything in life seriously, and what I wish to say rather is that one day, for the first time in ages, I'd most certainly like to take a gleeful ride in a cart bedecked with birch boughs once again, to sleep in a bed with a woven birch headboard, and to whip all the woes from my shoulders with a birch whisk in the sauna.

"It is darn difficult to tell you about birches when you, tiger, haven't seen the days they turn yellow nor witnessed the riotous fire of an autumn forest – how the leaves glow, radiant; how they twirl down before you and how the hollering storks pass by, high in the bleak sky.

"Yet even you comprehend life's eternal cycle, birth and death, though you haven't the slightest notion of a winter filled with snow flurries. And then, when the sky is broad and bare, the night long and dark, I'd like to sit inside, before the stove, and watch the little flame sprout; to see the way the logs crackle and burn; to stoke the fire and ultimately make peace with the fact that one day, everything will turn to cinder…

"In the morning, snow squeaks beneath your feet and bullfinches line the branches of the white birches like red poppies. I go on a long walk and take my time choosing a downy birch, because they have birds-eye rings and make you wonder what can be done with them…"

The great artist trailed off thoughtfully.

"I hear you, Eduard. It's a new and unfamiliar world for me, don't be angry. But I believe these birches of yours are quite wonderful things. Let them stand around me, then, if you praise them and yearn for them so.

"I consent."

The tiger maintained his pose, his paws crossed, and resembled a docile domestic cat. Yet it wouldn't pay to trust the tiger especially, because in truth, he longed even more dearly for his stomping grounds, hiding places, and watering holes.

For longings can never run out when they are longings for one's homeland.

1964

Translated by Adam Cullen

In the Eye of the Wolf
Helga Nõu

She recognises the back of his neck. A shiver or a shudder passes through her like an electric shock. That particular neck, two rows forward – she could have picked it out from thousands. The straight, strong, and stubborn dark hair that grew in a spiral on the neck, not vertically like anyone else's, but horizontally, from left to right. And that little pale, or rather grey blotch above the left ear where the hair lacked pigment for some reason: who else had such a mark right there? The furrow with the artery that throbbed between the neck muscles, the reddish-brown birthmark (though it had lightened over the years) in the shadow of his collar, the angular earlobe, the sharp jut of the jawbone, the selfish posture of the shoulders: everything!

After twenty-six years – or had even more gone by? The neck seems as vigorous as it ever was, he hadn't greyed yet. How was that possible? Had *he*, then, not aged in the meantime? Must only women age, wrinkle, become ugly? Even so. Changes to the neck, signs of the years, barely noticeable but present nonetheless, could be spotted upon closer inspection: the skin a little rougher, the muscles slightly slacker and not as smooth or flexible as before. Even judging from the slight rear angle, it wasn't impossible there could be a small fold beneath his chin.

Baltic Belles

The auditorium lights dim slowly and steadily, directing the audience's attention to the stage. It coaxes them out of everyday life and into a fantasy world: Watch, listen, and forget! For the price of your ticket, we offer you two and a half hours of oblivion. The play is old, but the production is new. Life repeats, is reborn anew every morning, and remains always and forever new, like the boar Sæhrímnir at the ancient Nordic Vikings' heavenly feast.

The curtain opens and a bright spotlight illuminates an actor in light-coloured clothing on stage. He extends a hand to the audience, inviting each and every one to come along with him to the events in some other time and reality. But the woman in the seventh row doesn't see him, doesn't see anything at all apart from the silhouette of the man sitting two rows ahead of her. She *is* already in another time, far from both the theatre and what is happening on stage. She is in her own story within her own reality, her own time.

She arrived when it was already ten minutes to three: yes, she could even remember the exact time. She hadn't wanted to wait conspicuously in the middle of the square, so pretended to study the shop windows. Shoes. Handbags. Cameras. She was actually the only one standing there; the only one, for whom time had appeared to halt. Everyone and everything else around her – the people, the trucks, the taxis – coursed past her as the rapid current of a noisy metropolis. Life, trash, and exhaust fumes. (Back then, she hadn't yet known that life itself is exhaust.) Thoughts? No, she had already made her decision and there was nothing more to think about. All was clear, even that she had betrayed her father with that decision.

Baltic Belles

Daughter, never, ever forget that you are a member of our tenacious and ambitious nation. If you compare yourself to your present surroundings, you see that most of your peers allow life to take whatever course it will, without aim or effort. One newspaper reported that seventy per cent of Swedish youth are too stupid to be able to continue their education. That's not an exaggerated figure, you know. You, however, have studied further and have acquired vastly greater knowledge. You possess the will and the ambition to advance. It is an intrinsic quality we Estonians are born with; one that we have been ingrained with over centuries. That is why you must remain loyal to your nation.

The cars, buses, and ordinary people in a hurry – they all rushed past her, hastening off to somewhere else. Young and old all jumbled together: no one stood still. And in truth she herself appeared to be only momentarily motionless, as she was similarly on her way somewhere else because of her decision.

Only her father was standing still – standing and looking back. He thrived on his pride and saw nothing else. In truth he didn't actually have much else, either, because with his Estonia-centric education there was nothing for him to do here in Sweden. Logging, later a packing job at a paint factory, and lastly working in solitude in a state institution's archive: that was his whole career. He had to find pride somewhere else: by being Estonian, fighting communism, and bringing a daughter up in the Estonian spirit. Like a caged animal, he roared in the zoo of exile and refused to eat the tasty food he was served, even though it was enriched with vitamins. Instead, he did his utmost to disparage his benefactors behind their backs at every opportunity:

"We must not give up or blend with the stupid and degenerate Swedish nation! Look for yourself: there are imbeciles at every turn!"

"Dad, I'm an adult and I know what I'm doing. Roland is no imbecile. He's from a good family. His father has a degree, just like you. And he himself studies…"

"That so-called Swedish university is no university! We had a real university back in Estonia. Here, there's just a school of slightly higher education with no organisation or aims or anything. You attend for a couple of years, and that's it. And as I recall, that hooligan of yours dropped out."

"Roland's found work now, but he'll continue his studies afterward, naturally. Later."

"Later – as if! Swedes lack ideals, they lack character."

"You don't even know Roland well enough to comment on his character…"

"It's a question of principle and now, this conversation is over!"

"It's like you're from the last century, when fathers determined whom their daughters had to marry. As long as he was rich!"

"And rightly so! But we're talking about intellectual richness here."

The worst part was that she understood her father. But there was nothing to be done: she had to choose. And she chose Roland, would have chosen him at any time and in any situation. Roland was like poison in her blood, yes – in her entire body.

Her heart ached, ached *physically*. It tingled just like the other body inside of her, whose name was to be Ulrika. She couldn't feel her yet, no – only her breasts were tender. Father would have died of shame, had he known.

Just eight minutes left, then seven.

She hadn't carried on the argument with her father because there would be no point. It was their eternal struggle; a game, in which they both knew exactly what the rules were. Mum never intervened. She supported her husband in principle, but did try to soften the situation, for the most part. In her own wordless way, she was both a mother and motherly; more body and intuition than principle. Till this point, the struggle with her father had been limited to words and neither of them had crossed the line. But now, she herself had gone across it – outside the game. She no longer had control over the situation or her own emotions. The game had gotten out of hand, and she was faced with an inevitable ultimatum. She had to make a choice. The chance the urine test was incorrect was miniscule.

And *he* should be coming soon: the one for whom she was waiting. *He*, who had penetrated his way first into her, then into her family, and finally into the whole "Estonian spirit", in the wake of which not one notion was the same anymore. Now, *he* was also to become a part of her future: that had been her decision, and now, soon, in six minutes, they were to meet. They had agreed on the time and place. Now, soon, in five minutes...

It probably hadn't even crossed her mind that the one she was waiting for might not show up, though a fear of it nested in her heart the whole time: that was probably the reason why it ached. And the woman waiting stared at the items on display in the shop windows again – the colourful glasses, bowls, and vases – without actually seeing them. Anticipation bounced off the glass and reflected only herself. Four minutes left, then three minutes, then two. She had thought everything out carefully: the words that were soon to gush over her lips and join them together for good. Happy, warm words in a cold, strange city.

It was drizzling, yes – she remembers clearly.

The anticipation gnawed at her. The public square and the uniform, impassive, streaming crowd reflected in the glass. School boys, shoppers carrying tote bags, a few people leaving work early for home, one cute couple holding hands. Her heart fluttered painfully in her chest. Suddenly, someone appeared to stop... was it *him*? No, a stranger behind her craned to inspect something in the shop window, then continued on his way. The next one? Not him, either. No one has any reason to show up to a rendezvous before the agreed-upon hour. Nevertheless, the woman waiting knew even before the clock in the church tower struck its three hollow times: she knew the one she was waiting for would not come. Dong, dong, dong. Three strikes. Three like a court sentence. The asphalt glinted damply as teardrops streamed down the windshields of the parked cars, trickled down their metal bodies, and collected in black puddles in the gutters.

She kept waiting, of course. Stiff from fear, cold, and humiliation, she waited five minutes, then ten. She waited a quarter hour, then half. Yet the sentence had been declared and the time no longer held any significance.

There was a telephone box on the far side of the square. What if maybe... the frail and naïve stalk of hope grew into a great and mighty tree with astonishing speed. Something must

Baltic Belles

have come up! Something happened that prevented him from coming. Pride and self-respect endeavoured to raise protest, but the state of unknowing is harder to endure than anything else, and even before she'd really considered the situation or come to any decision, she found herself standing in the cramped, filthy box reeking of cigarette smoke and gripping the cold bakelite receiver in fingers that were just as cold. A silver coin bearing the profile of the Swedish king clinked its way into the ebony-black device and she dialled six familiar digits on the rotary's finger wheel. This was followed by the crackling of the connection and then ringtones: first, second, third, fourth. She couldn't bear to hear any more and slammed the receiver down on the hook, closed her eyes, and rested her head against the graffitied wall. How long she stood like that, she couldn't tell, but a foreign sound was what ultimately pierced her consciousness. She fluttered her eyes open and startled: on the other side of the dirty square pane, pressed tight against the glass, was the gawking face of a stranger.

"Do you plan to talk or is the telephone free?" a gruff voice asked.

"Yes... no, I was just about to make a call!"

She hurriedly dug the unused silver krona out of the coin slot and, without actually considering her intentions, dropped it back into the device. She dialled the same number and listened to the piercing signals: first, second... then a bright, melodic woman's voice picked up.

Her entire past condensed into a single neck. A neck and nothing else. Flesh and hair. Even from several metres away, from two rows back, she can feel the bristly hairs on that neck,

Baltic Belles

can smell the mingled scent of tobacco and skin, can almost even taste it.

Somewhere far away in another land, they say there lives an old woman who collects wolf bones. She looks high and low for them, gathering them from the mountaintops and dried riverbeds, and when she finally has a complete wolf skeleton, she lays it out in front of her as a beautiful white sculpture. Then, she sits down by the fire and wonders what song to sing. And when she knows what song to sing, she stands and extends her arms over the wolf bones, and starts singing. She sings and sings until the wolf's ribs and its paws and its whole body is covered with flesh and fur. And she sings until the animal grows strong, its body twitches and its tail curls up and it starts to breathe. The woman sings until the wolf finally opens its eyes and rises onto its legs. And the old woman keeps on singing. She sings so loudly that the land trembles and the mountains and the valleys echo with it. And the wolf sprints across the bottom of the valley and runs faster and faster until it transforms mid-run – whether from the fast pace or leaping into a frothy river or the rays of sunlight or moonlight that strike its furry sides at a right angle, we do not know for certain. It transforms into a laughing young woman who runs off into the distance.[3]

Yet, the story being acted out on stage is Nordically chill and entirely dissimilar: women cannot be granted liberty, because they'll then turn into werewolves and slaughter the herd. Therefore, women must be kept in check. No flirting or idling away the time! No running around. *Keep in mind,*

---

[3] Based on *Women Who Run with the Wolves: Myths and Stories of the Wild Woman Archetype* by Clarissa Pinkola Estés.

daughter... the body is evil and wolves are to be shot. Those are the morals. The soil obliges us, and one cannot run from obligation. *We will carry on the ancient Estonians' struggle for the land they cultivated and defended with blood and toil...* obligation is a father's legacy to his children, his children's legacy to his grandchildren, and so on ad infinitum. *Our ancestors' tireless endeavour to have control over their own lives... Our nation has been ground to pieces and scattered to the winds once again. You, my daughter, must...*

Obligation. *Our nation...* like others, obligation had impeded him from living until it was too late. The woman in the seventh row can't follow what's happening on stage, doesn't even know what's playing or what is long-ago-lived or un-lived life. Who is she, herself? Her heart throbs, pounds, reminds her of forgotten longing; of long-past passion, pain, and humiliation. When does love turn into hatred? And that's far from all: the very worst is the crime that weighs heavy on her soul. Who is to blame for that? She alone? No, not she alone. Did anyone force her to do it? Who? Dad is dead and the dead can no longer be blamed for anything. What's more, he wasn't the one who forced her, but rather that, or those, whom he represented. The Estonian people? Oh, go to hell, the lot of you! The neck there, two rows ahead.

The woman breathes rapidly, her face flushed. Shouldn't she, after all these years, forgive and forget already? Who knows: maybe she *has* forgiven, but not forgotten. No, never! Neither has she forgiven. Whom? That man, of course! For what?

Very few know anything about the whole story, if anyone at all. No one cares either – why should they? A modest, laconic woman who lives a quiet life in her two-room suburban apartment without disturbing anyone is of interest to no one. One of the neighbours thinks she works at a library somewhere. A Balt, another might say. An Estonian or a Latvian – you can never tell the difference; it's just hard to remember. And, all in all, is it really of any importance? Those little countries.

Who is she, that middle-aged or slightly older woman, who bought a ticket for a seventh-row seat at the Stockholm City Theatre that night? That, we still don't know. What a neighbour can tell you or what the ticket vendor sees visibly is merely an outer shell; an outline, into which she has been stuffed and has finally hardened, almost petrified. Only occasionally, very rarely, will some part of her former self still work its way into her veins through the door of subconscious, causing her blood to surge, to turn hot once more. It proves that she's still alive and that everything isn't utterly over, regardless. And in those instances, she awakens almost with a sense of amazement and feels that if there were still a chance, then she would be prepared to break the rules again. Wolf-woman, wanderer, predator, killer, pursued, killed, Tiina. That is her earthly name: Tiina. And she was born a daughter of the earth.

The woman in the seventh row of the Grand Auditorium of the Stockholm City Theatre suddenly feels a strong throbbing tension in her lower abdomen: one akin to pain. And she muses that if she were male, she would have an erection.

She inclines forward, further and further, and without anyone noticing, she nimbly leaps two rows ahead, up to the man. She presses herself against him, sitting on his lap. She wraps herself around the man's chest and body and plants her lips on his bristly neck. First as a kiss: firm, soft, and moist. She inhales through her nostrils, taking in the tanned skin that smells of sweat and tobacco, as intoxicating as it ever was, but more sensual and maddening than ever before. And all at once, she remembers more than she ever has in all those years. A strong, arousing tingling passes through her body. She searches and probes the man's jaw and mouth with hungry lips, lips that are hard and dry – she hasn't yet reached the source. But she knows: *you are here now, and you won't escape me again!*

The man isn't afraid, is yet unsuspecting. On the contrary: in his self-righteousness, in his manly vanity, he exposes his neck to the woman for her to kiss: drink me, marvel at me, adore me! The more, the better. I am your everything! Saliva mixes with saliva, body with body; they become one in the darkness and the shuddering world disappears around them. Theatre is life and life is theatre. On stage or not: who knows, and it doesn't really matter. Only once the woman has reached that most crucial vital artery – once she is absolutely sure she has found the exact right place – does she bare her teeth. She relishes the anticipation, relishes her triumph. Cautiously, she sinks her teeth into the man's neck, and can already taste the inebriating tang of warm blood. She sucks and sucks. The man still doesn't react; in his hubris, he still doesn't sense or believe the gravity of the situation, but rather regards the pain as gratification. And the woman is spurred on by fresh impetus and, with an abrupt and powerful jerk, rips open his throat. The blood gushes and the man slumps, gurgling, into his seat.

The next day, the headline of the sensational front-page story in the newspapers is: *THEATRE ATTENDANT SLAUGHTERED DURING SHOW. Last evening, a man's body was found in the audience of the drama "The Bite", which was performed in the Stockholm City Theatre's Grand Auditorium. According to identification found in the deceased's pocket, the man was 52-year-old Roland Annersten of Huddinge. Having inspected the bite marks and injuries sustained to the deceased's neck, the police and coroners who were called to the scene determined the cause of death to be a yet-unknown and uncaptured predator that ripped open the victim's throat. The fact that no one else in attendance witnessed the bloodthirsty killer, nor noticed anything else unusual during the performance, remains a mystery to police. Theatre staff and ushers did not remark any mysterious creature, either, nor have any footprints or traces of the beast been found. The bloody and exceptionally savage killing must have been committed during the play's final act, as according to several witnesses, the victim was alive and well during the intermission. Also remarkable is the coincidence of the play's title, "The Bite", which is a modern rendition of the drama "The Werewolf" by the Estonian playwright August Kitzberg. The police investigation is ongoing.*

1999

Translated by Adam Cullen

Tango
Eeva Park

Borru rang and invited me to a dance class.

He said if I didn't come I shouldn't even hope to get out of the corner and onto the ballroom floor at the next New Year's Eve party.

He's so lovely. Honestly, he's one of the nicest people in the whole of Tallinn: when he meets you on the corner of Harju Street or Vana-Posti Street, he opens his arms wide and greets you, as if he'd dreamed of you the previous night and then spoken about it to his Valda over morning coffee. Because he can tell Valda everything, and he does; Valda is his muse, just like my friend Gala is the muse of Salvador.

He is also the only one among those dopey Estonians who is sure to wave back at you and hurry across the street to meet you. Last time we bumped into each other, he bought, right there by the fence of the conservatoire, some early hepaticas – short-stemmed, smelling of moss – from an old Estonian woman, and gave them to me. Standing in the middle of a dark, muddy puddle, he eulogised the spring so that even the flower seller got all excited, as if that short, skinny Borru, hopping around like a sparrow, had given the flowers to her, not to me. The old woman even smiled from under her faded and dented felt hat, wished us a Happy Easter in advance and then was shocked when I responded in Estonian. They realise immediately, after a couple of words, that I'm a foreigner after all, and the flower woman probably got scared that I would go and report both her unlicensed flower selling and the fact that she had mentioned the forbidden holiday. What a fool – I'm not even Russian, but she grabbed her basket and hurried away at full gallop, probably to the Viru gates or beyond the railway station, where among all sorts of other stuff flowers are sold, too. The militia might try to keep an eye on them, but just you try to ban trading in a city with so many nooks and crannies.

And the people are desperately poor: they're selling off valuable old furniture and children's boots too, both moth-ridden fur coats and table services dug out after the war, and almost none of them buys art, let alone has an artist paint their portrait.

Borru didn't notice anything then, or if he did, he didn't let it bother him. He knows that I have no connections with the KGB, although naturally I'm a member of the Party, because what's the point of not being a member now they're in power?

Borru was in Chelyabinsk during the war – this is where we got acquainted, in fact. I made many other acquaintances there, but now, here in Tallinn, it feels that several of my great friends from that time remember nothing, since they've returned home. From one year to the next they feel increasingly embarrassed to recognise me in front of those flower women and passers-by, even though their memory seems all right when they happen to meet me somewhere at the Union.

Borru invited me and so I joined the course, but as I had no one else to take along as a partner, I asked my model – a leading shipyard worker – to accompany me to the first lesson at least. He didn't want to, so I paid him for his company with a fancy Armenian brandy brought back from Moscow, but that wasn't much good. Apart from that, this gracious, long-legged star worker lacked any sense of rhythm; he lacked it so completely that the dance teacher came to us every now and then and, loudly counting one, two, three, one, two, three, finally asked if the comrade is aware that dance is a walk of life in which the man must lead the lady.

"But she won't let me," comrade Ronk replied, staring at the floor, and everybody laughed, me included, because I felt sorry about the brandy and he had trodden on the toes of my left foot really painfully, twice.

He was sweating terribly; rivulets of sweat were running down his forehead into his straight pitch-black eyebrows, and when the music started again, he pushed me across the floor like a rag doll. During the break, when vodka tempered with redcurrant squash was passed around, he went to the toilet for a moment and never came back. I sighed with relief, but Borru's wife announced that she knew an excellent partner for me, who could replace my fled Prince Charming in the next lesson.

"Ülo is a good lad, although he hasn't got your Hercules' musculature. But he's got legs and he wants to dance, too, or so he said anyway."

I tried to explain that the other one had only been a model sent for the factory mural, but everybody kept mocking me: apparently, they knew very well that I walked round among the workbenches like in a slave market, looking for the most attractive male models.

"No reason to be ashamed – if you're given a chance, you must keep your eyes peeled," Leevandi the graphic artist said.

"If some handsome hunk is offered on top of the fee, there's no need to pretend that athletic beauty means nothing to us. Well, broad shoulders and proper buttocks are surely not some bourgeois relic... It is precisely our job to paint the working people walking towards socialism looking so beautiful that they themselves will believe in their own beauty. Try to put some skinny or bald one into the Honour-to-Work-poster – it won't do. Although the world is full of decent baldies, a Stakhanovite must have broad shoulders and bushy curls, otherwise you will find yourself in the bin, along with your poster."

"Don't give him any more squash. He can go and riot at the café Kuku if he likes, but one needs a clear head and steady step at the dance lesson," Borru said, taking his Valda into a tight grip and leading her truly skilfully into swift tango movements.

The dance teacher and his wife Anu – I was told in whispers that they were the best ballroom dancing pair in Estonia – showed us the steps with supreme grace and élan. The man with his body taut as a spring of steel, and the woman's light, gliding moves gave the dance a deceptively simple and logical delineation, but no one could follow it instantly, even those who considered themselves good dancers. Counting rhythm, the dance teacher watched the colliding pairs and then said that with us it was clear he needed to start with the basics. He didn't even seem to notice the offended murmur, the muted cries of complaint coming from the most maladroit dancers; he laughed when Leevandi said that he'd been the boy who was most in demand at every village dance. And he ordered us – me too, having been abandoned by my partner – out of our seats, into a line against the wall, making us, the men behind him and the women behind Anu, follow their steps slowly and accurately.

Now he was training us just four or five steps at a time, making us repeat them again and again. Then he turned on the music and told us to show him if we'd understood anything at all.

"Work your knees! You can't dance tango without switching on your knees! Feel your bodies, feel the rhythm – step, step, turn, promenade... as if you were carrying a suitcase in each hand, go lower... have you never carried your paint box? This step is called the swivel, but you've got a long, long way to go before you get there."

"Very good," the dance teacher's wife said to me when I was trying out the steps on my own, and I felt a hot surge of joy, which subsided only when the dance teacher used me to show what strange positions we women can assume when dancing: "What are you trying to find on the floor? Do you dance with your legs or with your head? What's the organ controlling your movements? The toes? Ladies, straighten up and just dance with your partners: what's the hurry all the time? You are being led, not the other way round, just this once..." he explained, and everyone was overjoyed when my legs knotted up completely and I only stayed upright by grabbing hold of the dance teacher.

"Well, well, well..." he said, standing up steadily as if having known in advance that at some point I would fall. "Close contact with the partner must be maintained, of course, but in an upright position and moving to the rhythm."

I got angry, hearing the others laughing, and for that very

reason decided that if Valda did indeed persuade this Ülo the watercolourist to be my partner, I'd go and learn at least this one dance and dance it at the Artists' Union party in absolutely the correct tango fashion, those creeping tango steps, those damn swivels, a suitcase in each hand. I'd dance all the turns and promenades without a partner.

Ülo came and was only interested in the waltz, which he wanted to learn to surprise his bride at the wedding party. He twirled me so enthusiastically that I got dizzy and my leather-soled shoes felt so dangerously slippery despite the powder sprinkled onto the floor, that I went to the shoemaker and had proper dance shoes made for me, with suede soles. Noting them instantly, the dance teacher gave me an attentive look, nodding and saying that some of us, apparently, were close to getting the point. I wanted to tell him that my partner's exuberance at the wedding waltz on the slippery floor had made me think I was going to break my neck, but as this top dancer was a man whose remarks even shut Leevandi's mouth, I was only happy that I managed to smile quietly.

At the same time, I wanted some recompense for the price of the handmade shoes. I'm not half as well-paid an artist as is generally thought. For example, for the portrait series of the state leaders commissioned by the Ministry of Fisheries I was partly paid in smoked eel, which, admittedly, I sold to acquaintances for a decent price. But as I'm planning, with a permit acquired from the Union, to buy a car as soon as possible, I keep an accurate record of my incomings and outgoings. A single woman without male support cannot afford too much, not even in order to learn the tango. Everything that once belonged to my grandparents here in central Tallinn has been

Baltic Belles

nationalised and, luckily for me, nobody any longer knows that in a different era both a haberdashery shop in Viru Street and a lingerie factory in Kalamaja would have been part of my inheritance. Mine and my brother's, in fact, but he was killed during the first summer of the war and is now protecting me far better than one would have thought possible when he was still eating my sweets up. Life is strange, my great-grandfather said when my mother took us to his home and he wondered every time whose children were walking round his flat.

When now I pass his house and look at the sign of a government office parading on its wall, I wonder exactly the same thing.

"You should sit for a painting," I said to the dance teacher's wife, grey-eyed Anu. "Wouldn't you want to sit for me? No, no, not for a nude study; for a portrait."

"Me?" she asked, and for some reason laughed.

"Why not? You're young and beautiful, a well-known ballroom dancer... I am a portrait painter renowned throughout the Soviet Union. Several of my works are being exhibited in Moscow."

"You know, I don't care for it somehow. Where would I put this portrait? People would think I'm in love with myself," the young woman said, and then announced to people as they left, "next week we're competing, so Monday's class is not happening. But you're all welcome to watch the international Baltic Cup for ballroom dancing. I believe it might still be possible to get tickets, although the performers will be coming from as far as Poland."

Borru's Valda came to a halt – she's always keen to go everywhere – but Lehti Keerd, who had given the dance teacher and her wife one of her graphic works, thanked her very politely and added that if she were Anu, she would think twice before refusing such an offer of a portrait. In the future, decades later, it might feel a shame that she hadn't got herself immortalised by a renowned artist.

This Keerd is a very peculiar person, I decided, because I even saw two reasons for her surprising help and kindness. Firstly, she might have hoped that thanks to a new commission I would hand over my position in the car queue to her and her husband; or perhaps she thought that by painting a portrait I wished to make a gift to the dance teacher and his wife.

"A painting is not a reproduction that you can hand out for petty cash," I later said to Borru as we walked across Town Hall Square, but he reassured me that this Keerd had certainly not meant that.

"She just wished to support your offer and give you proper recognition," Borru asserted, warmly as ever, and supported my arm when I lost my footing for a moment. The high heel of my boot, which I'd bought at the GUM department store in Moscow, had got wedged between the cobbles, and although I'd rather have broken my leg, the heel broke off. When I limped on homewards from there, I wept angry tears for the rough streets of this city without caring what the passers-by thought. When are they going to replace the cobbles in some of those Karja streets with asphalt? I decided to raise this question at the next meeting, and I know that all the ladies will agree with me, anyway. One day the Dark Ages must end, even in this city.

When we gathered at the dance class again, it turned out that Borru, together with Valda and some of the others, had gone to see our teacher and his partner competing, and were now congratulating them on winning the tournament. To conclude the course they had brought flowers, sparkling wine, and Ülo – perhaps in the hope of getting some extra lessons for his wedding waltz – had given the couple a totally decent watercolour painted on a Saaremaa beach. When I once again mentioned the portrait during a break, the dance teacher's wife suddenly agreed to sit, and the following day she was standing in my studio, wearing a blue blouse buttoned up to the throat.

"No," I said, glancing at her. "I won't paint you like this. What is this about blue now? Everybody comes in blue or grey, thinking that's what's beautiful. Well, it isn't! Your complexion is pale enough – why turn yourself entirely into a whitewashed wall? Colour, colour is needed – otherwise you'll look just like this city."

"Blue goes with my eyes, that's what everybody says," this dance teacher of mine announced. But now I let her know that eye colour doesn't matter, that skin is everything, the skin tone determines all the other colours, not hair colour, never mind the eyes, and this is why all Estonian women look so dull and the same – because they know nothing about colours.

"What are you afraid of?" I asked, grabbing a red sash and throwing it over her shoulders. "As a dancer you should know that first impressions count."

"First impressions, yes… but you also have to know the steps and keep the rhythm, or you'll ruin the impression," she replied, taking off the sash and glancing at the city view on the easel.

"Try this," I told her and handed over a bright green

silk sash.

"Well, this certainly isn't my colour," she said when I pushed her in front of the big mirror hanging on the wall.

"Choose something from here then, we'll look together," I suggested, opening the door of the cupboard and producing a few more pieces.

"You've got a whole fabric shop here," the dance teacher's wife said, and finally agreed to wear a dark pink shawl.

"Quite a different story," I said. "Now I can see you much more precisely… this way I can paint you and you can look yourself. Yes, this is good, this is excellent, now don't move…"

I painted. The woman's face was more interesting taken into separate parts than I had expected, and in only a couple of hours I knew that this was a success. In only two intense sittings I almost completed the portrait, but when I then said that by the following sitting the work would be finished and named the price, the woman looked at me with surprise and said she didn't know.

"What don't you know?" I asked.

"I misunderstood… you wanted to paint me, you demanded…"

"I made a suggestion," I said.

"If it's alright, I'll bring my husband along and he will say…" she muttered a bit unclearly.

"Yes, by all means," I said, quite confident that I'd get a sale.

But two days later, when the dance teacher and his wife were standing in my study, he took a look at the portrait placed on the easel and said, "What do I need it for?"

"What do you mean, what for?"

"I haven't commissioned it," he said, with the confidence that was also in his dancing. He turned around and, together with his wife, walked out of my studio.

Next time I saw Borru, he was painting the view of the city gate in Pikk Jalg. I turned round and went down the stairs of Lühike Jalg instead, but then my annoyance passed and later, at the Mireille Mathieu concert, I was happy to see him and Valda walking in the foyer at the Estonia Concert Hall. It turned out that the music of Mathieu had become a shared passion for me and Valda; that we both admired her young voice and dark hair, just the way both of us loved Piaf more than anyone. Borru had somehow, who knows where from and for what price, got Valda a copy of Mathieu's record, which I of course didn't have, but then I promised to get backstage, whatever it took, and talk to the singer herself. Valda laughed her purring throaty laugh and said that if I succeeded, if I really could show her Mireille's autograph on the programme, she would be prepared to eat her old boots and give the record to me.

Well, I did get backstage. Considering that a relative on my mother's side worked in the office there, it was not surprising, and as there were some people constantly crowding round the door of Mathieu's dressing room, I managed to push through and, having got to the door and found it ajar, slip into the room. Now I made two short steps forward, handed Mathieu a white rose and said the first few sentences in French that came into my mind. Her suntanned, black-eyed child-like face momentarily lost its polite smile, she became clearly excited and asked me if I really spoke French.

"Oui, mademoiselle," I replied, taken aback by the glances

Baltic Belles

around me, but victoriously at the same time, and then told Mathieu about my trip to Paris with my parents. Mireille told me that she was not a *Parisienne*, but instead from Avignon, although she loved Paris, and then she asked if the following day I'd like to show her round Tallinn.

"I've got a couple of hours to spare, and it would be good to speak French to a local person," she explained, rattling away so fast that it was hard to follow her. The Intourist guide, who was standing next to us, stared at me blankly, but I nodded and said to the man that naturally I'd be happy to join them the following day, adding in Russian that I'm an artist, a member of the Artists' Union, and that I'm in the Party.

The guide pretended not to be interested, but when Mireille turned to him, he was forced to tell me a moment later to come to the hotel foyer at ten the following morning.

I was ten minutes early and just moments later Mireille Mathieu appeared in a black raincoat, black sunglasses and a funny little headscarf tightly tied. To my surprise she announced that we could go out into the town straightaway. I would rather have waited for the guide, but when she walked impatiently out of the door, I took her directly to Toompea. Soon we were standing side by side on the viewing platform looking down at the port, and at the red tiled roofs and Pikk Jalg below us, where Borru had just recently set the legs of his easel between the cobbles. And then I remembered the boot heel that had come off in Town Hall Square, and that I'd never be able to get another pair of such boots.

"Would you like to see how Soviet artists live? Would you like to come to my studio?" I asked before I could even think what I was doing.

Baltic Belles

She looked at me for a moment, then said that she'd be happy to come, and asked, pointing with her hand, what the arch-like building far off on the seashore was.

I explained, looking towards the Song Festival Stage, that this is the place where local people gather to sing, and then asked, still unable to believe, where she'd like to go, and she laughed and said to my studio, of course.

For the whole time I was afraid that someone would come up to us, that a black car would stop beside us and the angry guide and some other men would clamber out of it, but even when I looked back there was nobody to be seen, only a drunk came out of the yard of a collapsing old building as we passed it, setting off down the hill behind us, clinking his bag of empty bottles. The city smelled of dust and the dark corner on the stairs of Lühike Jalg stank of piss, but Mireille didn't notice any of this. Instead she stroked the huge riveted door in the stone wall and wanted to know if it was medieval.

I answered, "Oui, mademoiselle," because I was more and more worried about the ceaseless clinking of glass behind us.

When a couple of school girls came running up the stairs towards us, my mind eased a bit for some reason. Mireille made a couple of light hopping steps and said that she liked this city, that it was so quiet and old that it reminded her of Avignon, where she used to live together with her father, mother and thirteen siblings up till her fifteenth birthday, in such a shack, a house that wanted to fall apart every time the wind blew.

"It was wonderful that it stayed up," she said. "But it was even more wonderful to have a bath for the first time."

"What?" I asked, thinking that I'd misunderstood. But while we were walking towards my studio, she told me that before they moved to the new flat with a bath, she didn't only look after her little brothers and sisters, but she also kept the floor of their home, with its dripping roof and decaying walls, so clean at all times that one could've eaten one's dinner off it.

I hadn't cleaned my studio and when we stepped in she said that all this was exactly like in a film. I pushed my socks and the sandwich plate under the sofa and started to show her my paintings. She nodded, regarding them, then stepped to the window and said that I'd got an amazing view.

This is when I suggested to her that she take as many paintings from my studio as she wished, and to send me a pair of boots from France for them. Standing by the window, she glanced at me over her shoulder and asked, "Boots?... what kind?"

"High-heeled, size 38, black... they go with anything," I explained and told her how, on the cobbles of Tallinn, I'd broken the heel of my boots bought at GUM in Moscow.

She didn't seem to listen, walking restlessly around the study, shifting pictures, lifting them to her eyes and putting then back by the wall. Finally she selected three paintings: quite an old one, a self-portrait made right after the war; one with a child holding a ball; and then the picture of the dance teacher's wife Anu, which I'd pushed behind the draft of a factory mural. Mireille didn't tell me why she wanted these ones, only looked out of the window once more, asked for a glass of water, took a wary sip from it, stuck the piece of squared note paper I'd written my address on into her coat pocket and said that she had to go back now.

"But the paintings?" I asked, as I couldn't possibly ask when and how soon she intended to send me the boots.

"The paintings will be picked up," she said, smiling and putting on the sunglasses, which had been hanging off her white blouse showing between the flaps of the coat.

This time we walked in front of the Art Hall, up the stairs onto the hill of Harjumägi, and although I was telling her the names of the buildings surrounding Victory Square, where the grandstand for the May and October parades is located, she didn't seem to be listening any longer. But as we were passing the cannon tower Kiek in de Kök, she stopped and said that she loved stones, her father being a stonemason.

"I miss my family," she said, "although God is near me always and everywhere. Today He is with me in this city."

"Oui," I said, wondering, why she was telling me such things.

"Don't you sense how close He is? Just here, just now?" Mireille continued and seemed surprised when I, panting on the slope, quickened my step and went ahead of her.

When we reached the hotel, the guide was standing by the front door, and the expression on his face made me certain that he already knew where we'd been. Perhaps there was a camera in the bottle bag so they could take photos unnoticed, or the schoolgirls storming up the steps were in fact young female officers, or my downstairs neighbour reported us the very moment we passed his door, because anyway it seemed to me that he always had his eye on me.

But then, this wasn't important as long as they knew where the foreign visitor was.

And the main thing was that the black-eyed girl didn't lose my address, which she had so carelessly stuck into her pocket.

The paintings were collected from my study only an hour later. They were taken by two men, who thoroughly examined them, broke open my properly framed self-portrait, and then fixed it immediately, on the spot, with the glue they'd brought, putting it into a plywood box along with the other pictures. The box was sealed in my presence, I saw how Mireille's name was written onto it, and I signed three ready-typed forms.

But the boots never arrived. I don't believe that Mireille failed to send them; this I don't believe. But maybe that package, too, was broken open, the heels were broken off and they looked between the soles and couldn't put them back together after that, because Parisian boots can't be cobbled together just like that.

About ten years later, on a stuffy and dusty evening in spring, the wife of my dance teacher came to me wanting to purchase the portrait with the pinkish violet scarf, which I had painted of her. She thought I might not even remember this painting of the grey-eyed woman with the dark pink silk shawl, and told me that they now had a bigger flat, where it would go very nicely, but I lifted the gramophone needle onto the beginning of the record, scratched and worn as it was, listened to Mireille's voice and said, "You're too late. Too late... that painting is in Avignon now and I can't paint another like it."

2006

Translated by Eva Finch and Jason Finch

In the Winds of Blue Heights
Mari Saat

I love leather. But not in the way leather artists typically do. And many people in general – I have noticed that people like leather: if only they had the money, they would wear leather jackets, waistcoats and coats, would sit in leather armchairs and stroke leather book covers. That leaves me indifferent – perhaps I like fabric even better, particularly linen, the smell of canvas, tow cloth, canvas... yes, compared to all other materials, such as wood, fabric, paper, leather is even a bit distasteful to me.

But I like the skin of a live human. Especially white, delicate, smooth skin like that of the inner arm, where the blood vessels shine through. – Live skin actually glows, because it radiates the warmth of the blood. Well, it seems that way to me, at least!

I have also felt the skin of a dead body – and jumped back with a start, although it was my mother's, and I was not at all afraid of the dead, let alone of my own mother, and I did not feel unable to stay alone with her, after touching her, even at night in the chapel at the graveyard; just the cold claylike shell that my mother's form was now covered in felt strange. Because dead skin is indeed like damp clay, heavy and cold, and its colour is not vivid. It feels like if you happen to press it harder, a fingerprint will stay in it just like in clay... and maybe it's true that it does.

When you cover scarlet red in white, it gives the same sensation as live skin... I have thought that for some time, when I'm rich enough, I could make some such thing – a sofa or an armchair, which would be such a light, smooth, glowing thing, perhaps even heated from inside, against which you could feel like you do against a live human...

Curiously, everybody I've told about such a piece of furniture sees it completely differently from me! – They find it creepy, horrid, like something out of a Hitchcock film... it was only Emil who didn't shiver at it. Although even he saw it differently: to his mind it was erotic – he started to laugh and said that it reminded him of my father's definition of an ideal woman: in father's opinion a true woman must be such that she could smother the man between her breasts... this, of course, isn't my father's original thought but some saying – Russian or Ukrainian. But all men seem to like it for some reason. But in fact, my mother was small and delicate, thin rather than plump. I am not as fine-boned, but still remain really far from this "true woman".

But as for the sofa, Emil thought that lying on it he would feel exactly that, especially if it was heated as well... I should take Emil's opinion into account because above all Emil loves warmth. Warmth, cleanliness, beauty, deliciousness...

Should I say 'loves' or 'loved'?

And as for father, I couldn't remotely say if he still 'loves' something or 'loved'; if he still 'wants' something or 'wanted', and when the doorbell rings and my father stands there in front of me, whether it is my real father under whose skin warm live blood is glowing... or instead a hallucination or even a zombie with a skin cold like clay... that I could believe of him – the latter, that he could even rise from the grave and come back, if he was determined to do that...

Father and Emil got along pretty well – the one time they met – although they didn't understand a word each other said. Perhaps this is why they got along: because it wasn't possible for them to talk – only as much as I saw fit to interpret.

And that they never managed to meet again... so far, at least – to put it more accurately.

Then they had nothing better to do than to start playing chess – blitz chess, because father couldn't stand (or can't stand?) to concentrate too long... '*Blitzkrieg!*' – as father liked to say – this was a favourite expression in his sparse foreign vocabulary, and such that it is probably understood by everybody of his age; at least Emil understood him right away when father shook the box of chess pieces next to his face and belligerently trumpeted, '*Blitzkrieg!*'

I wonder if all men can play chess? And what do they find in it? The ones who are my father and Emil's age all can, I think. But it seems that the younger ones can't any more. Although long, long ago it was a pastime of Indian ladies. Had my world become so degenerate that it could no longer take an interest in chess? Am I a degenerate compared to my father? Well, that I don't believe! Perhaps compared to the ladies of Ancient India, but not compared to father!

I actually grasp, although I don't get it myself, why chess can be of interest – after all, it combines possibilities to act. But I am not interested in that at all; I'm not at all interested in behaviour, acts, or even in Time; I am truly interested only in my completed works, the result. All the interim stuff, including the time, are only barriers that have to be surmounted between my thoughts and the completed work, and therefore everything else is something unpleasant and disturbing... but of course, I can't generalise – it's possible that the world would still be full of chess players if there were no computers now. Indeed, many of these potential chess players are simply players of computer games.

In any case, to my surprise Emil seemed to battle my father respectfully in this *Blitzkrieg*, and not get at all fed up – from time to time they even laughed loudly... how on earth does the human brain work if moving some standardised plastic pieces amuses it? I don't mean this in a judgmental way – it seems to me there's some secret here that I can't understand. Or can't be bothered to understand...

And at the same time they were complete opposites! Father was sturdy and stiff, as if he were only occasionally in the habit of personifying himself as a live human, and spent his real life, the larger part of it, as a bronze or granite bust of a military man. Even his coarse, straight black hair was closely smoothed down against his scalp and not a single hair of it would dare to stick up separately!

Emil was a lot taller and leaner than him, but seemed plump and soft in comparison. Also, his hair was soft and a bit wavy and therefore always looked slightly shaggy... father gave the impression that he scrubbed himself endlessly – and this is what he did, too; every morning he washed scrupulously in the cold shower and sprayed himself with cologne. I always kept some men's aftershave at home, in case father should pop in from his world travels, so he wouldn't then make the whole flat smell with his terrible colognes; he claimed that my aftershaves stank, but he accepted them all the same, he trusted me, at least here, in Estonia... Yes, but Emil, then, always felt clean, even when, at my behest, he didn't shave – I don't like beards, but I like it when one forgets to shave, occasionally, not always. Should this perhaps be categorised as an erotic desire? I don't know, in my opinion all categorisation is stupid. I simply like the variety – I also like to clean the flat in bursts, to let it get very messy and dusty and then to scrub it all day as if this was the last opportunity. This is also said to be the Russian way, at least to my grandmother's mind – in her opinion everything should be shining at all times. Perhaps she's right – meaning that this is the Russian way, because Emil also wanted to keep everything tidy around him, to put things exactly in their place. I noticed how he tried to put things back that often "dropped" behind me. But with him it didn't bother me; on the contrary, I sometimes tried to throw stuff around deliberately, so that quietly, unnoticed by me, or so he thought – because it seemed he feared giving offence by showing that he thought me sloppy – put them in their supposed places. Supposed – because at my place he could only guess where the right place for anything in particular might be: here things didn't have such strictly designated places as in his home... this amused me; at those times, he was like a gardener tidying up his flowerbeds after a hurricane and rainstorm, or even more – like a human in its highest sense, who has been called to this world to organise the wildness of nature...

He loved beautiful and delicious things – it was as if he ate mainly to admire flavours with his tongue; it was as if he was constantly looking for things to admire... of course, therefore, it must have been difficult for him here in Tallinn: mud or dust, depending on the weather, always accompany you here; and those houses, derelict, fungi-ridden, decaying, with peeling paint or crumbling plaster, rotten window frames – all this enters someone through their eyes and coils up there into a big grey gunk of depression, a ball of cobwebs like witches used to throw into people's mouths in olden times, so as to slowly kill them. Emil kept saying that all of it didn't bother him in the least, that he didn't even notice all this when I was with him – but in this respect I couldn't really believe him.

And of course, logically taken, this very sentence – when I'm with him – meant in fact that he accepted all of it thanks to me, but that otherwise it would bother him. And how long would I be able to protect him from all this misery? In reality, I no longer could, because immediately after Emilia was born he started to say that we should move to Sweden, that no 'beneficial environment' for a child existed here – for some reason this phrase upset me a lot, I could say it even enraged me, this extremely tactful-seeming phrase – as if it put me down, drawing some invisible yet impassable boundary between Emilia and us Estonians... yes, I wonder why this cautious phrase bothered me so much while his habit of putting stuff into order didn't? Maybe, if he'd chosen some other reason, if he had said, for example, that he found it difficult to be away from us, then I wouldn't have minded moving, even if I had guessed that this was not the only reason... or if he had just said frankly that everything here is dirty and derelict and he doesn't want his child to grow up here – then perhaps I might have fought back a bit and then given in... but 'unfavourable environment' – to my ears this is one of those typical Swedish expressions used to draw that invisible line

Baltic Belles

between oneself and the others, the more inferior ones. Very polite, near-invisible, but very inflexible... of course, we are all good at drawing lines; there is hardly a nation which is unable to find another one worse than itself, but not all can do it in such a sophisticated way.

I hate nations! Including us, Estonians! If I am even allowed to call myself an Estonian? But this is what I am, according to my passport, and above all I probably also think in an Estonian way. Because an Estonian is someone who thinks of themselves as Estonian, who draws the line between themselves and the nation of some of his or her ancestors and, being entirely honest, I can't remember ever, even in my childhood, allowing father to cross this line... what can I then blame Emil for, or other Swedes who are even more Swedish than him?

But at the same time, I don't feel that Estonia is my home – this place alone isn't sufficient for me. I feel that the world is my home! This might sound like ridiculous hyperbole. But in fact, if you look at it from high enough up, that isn't so. On the contrary: to feel this, you don't need to fly into space at all – you just have to lift your eyes. For that, a night in August works brilliantly. Just look at the tiny stars that are millions of times bigger than our world – at least this is what astronomers tell us... and this is what I sometimes think, that this little ball, this is enough for my home – I wouldn't want to leave here... although, to be precise, it's not so simple as just lifting your eyes and looking; at least it's not like that in the city – the city wants to put out the stars. Against the city lights the stars look dim, as if through a dirty pane of glass; even when you go to the beach or the park, the city is still above you with its brutal light. So it isn't that easy, after all – you have to travel out of the city on a cloudless night, and then the stars look real, as if they really existed; you might even feel that no instruments, spaceships or telescopes are needed, that you could charge into the star with your naked eye, if only you stayed still and kept looking with enough patience... the stars seem to be coming closer and closer, across the boundaries set by space – and more tangible...

This is why I dislike nations. They want to draw boundary lines! If they could, they would draw one between themselves and the wind. Then they would start trading with the air, or maybe export polluted air to poorer countries... it seems to me that it is the Earth we're chiefly unfair to when we divide it that way, and when I think about it I get bitter that I'm not a bird... or a soul; that I have a body which I have to move from one delineated area to another and, every time, to fill in some stupid forms and apply for a permit from some officials belonging to some gang that once conquered this piece of land and declared it their own. Because even if Estonians have lived here, exactly here, for seven thousand years, before that they still came here as a gang and killed the ones who were here before them! Somewhere inside me I feel that deep down within there is something older than the history of all these nations, and this something still remembers that time with no boundaries. And therefore, those boundaries offend it.

Perhaps it's only steppe peoples who feel this way, because it's possible that I've got the heart of a steppe person, although I don't want to admit it... one feels things with one's heart, right? Because I don't actually think this way. I think like a genuine Estonian – I don't want our small Estonia not

Baltic Belles

to have borders – as if not long ago it was torn off on one side and everyone could come and trample around on it as much as they liked... no, this I don't want, either – it is probably this Estonian sobriety that tells me to accept the inevitable, that the world is no longer a bare wilderness, that there are too many of us who we've wanted to be born here precisely at this end of the century and therefore we have to draw lines and borders and we have to have disputes and make war over little plots in this world...

Ah, I don't know! If I don't like boundaries, does that mean I shouldn't be sad about someone stepping out of the boundaries of their own body? Why does this sadden me endlessly? Do I pity the abandoned body? Or the soul, perhaps, that didn't even want to get free and is now wandering, confused, unable to find peace? Or do I instead pity myself?

I don't know about God. I can say nothing about him – I don't know him! Does He even exist? When I ask questions like this, no one answers?! But nobody can make me believe, either, that I have no soul, something that was alive before my body and will live on after that. I simply feel that it is so, no matter whether I think about it or not! And I think that the body, and particularly the face, is not just something shaped by nature and the parents' genetic code. No, those two are merely the material out of which someone, customarily referred to as soul, designs their exactly-fitting shell; this is how my father's body expressed (or expresses...) the other one who has shaped him and who is using him as their abode, and Emil's body, too, that other one – the true Emil...

"I see angels dancing in the wind..."

Why does this sentence haunt me? This isn't actually

a sentence, I guess, but a line from a poem? And I can't remember any more of it, not even where I read or heard it. Probably heard because when reading, one remembers better where something comes from – at least the cover of the book... I also have a feeling that this story or song said that the wind is the element of the angels, or the angels bring it about... but then again I seem to have heard that angels express themselves via water, for some reason via flowing water – is this not the reason why Muslims are so fond of flowing water, of fountains, decorating their gardens with those things?...

Only this sentence has started to pop up from time to time – to haunt me, as if a breeze carried it momentarily through my head, and this is disturbing... come to think of it, I don't even know whether it was: "I see angels dancing in the wind," or instead, "I see an angel dancing in the wind."

The latter version only differs by three letters but the meaning is completely different, at least to me: the former one is light and incandescent, the latter for some reason dark, one could even say threatening... in fact I know why it's like this – to say 'angels' plural is to generalise about someone or something that is generally considered good because it's associated with heaven and God; but one angel might be either one or the other – perhaps the one who was cast out of heaven, or the even more mysterious one – the angel of death, of whom no one really knows if he is one or the other... but, of course, other people might not see it like this – I just have my own personal relations with one angel...

Grandmother loved the uniform, but not just any uniform: the black one – the captain's uniform, as she said; the black uniform and the white scarf. I think this is the real reason why she disliked my father – it seems to me that she could have accepted everything else but not the fact that her granddaughter's father wore a green uniform, this symbol of a 'landlubber'. That if he had been Russian but with a black captain's uniform with gold epaulettes... such things matter very much to people, in fact... and it's to be suspected that she accepted Emil slightly more readily precisely for the reason that Emil came by ship, and that he loved sea travel but not aeroplanes. Yes, he didn't like aeroplanes, although he flew one to Paris or Cologne, but he preferred to come here by ship. He did not say that he was afraid of being in a plane crash; he said that the plane is cramped, that it depresses him... and he loved the sea... although he had nothing to do with either the black uniform or the seaman's occupation... (although in winter he wore a long dark coat and really beautiful long soft scarves – not white, to the dismay of grandmother, not even light-coloured, but still...)

In fact, Grandmother is no more childish in that matter than other people – they all have some norms in their heads that they like to comply with. For example, my friends and acquaintances, and I myself of course, because otherwise I'd have different friends and acquaintances, were definitely not in favour of my relationship with Emil. Marrying him would have been the worst of all – that would've been something like being elected to Parliament – something that no one can really blame you for, that you can always disguise with claims such as 'for my own state and people' or 'true love', but still... still it's as if you used some foul play to step into that 'more favourable environment'. But as my friends and acquaintances didn't believe it right to impose their convictions on others, they did not rub it in my face – moreover, if I'd decided because of that to stop having anything to do with Emil, it would've felt downright stupid... but actually I don't even think about such things when I am relating to someone; I'm not even able to think of such things when the person is right there before me. In my opinion, a person is somehow above all of the environments which they come from and those where they are, and their own values, even if they don't believe them, and holds on tight to those values...

And Emil, at least in my opinion, didn't love any norms or values – apart, perhaps, from this one time when he was considering Emilia's future... but in general, it seems to me that he was simply not interested in those things, that his paternal conscience simply awoke for a moment in relation to Emilia... because people exist who make an effort to violate norms and by that constantly remind themselves of those norms – those ones are the born rebels... but him?... yes, he did like order in things, but this was kind of different from imposing rules of conduct, this was more like creating beauty...

It seems to me (or I want to believe) that he thought about that more favourable environment just for a moment out of duty, because now he was a father and therefore sort of responsible... but in fact he was only interested in beauty and he regarded everything from that angle... it even seems to me that deep down he liked the global crisis in the art market, which he never tired of complaining about – that the average German had almost given up buying art and that France worked out barriers to protect domestic art; that somewhere deep down he was secretly happy that this way he wouldn't perhaps have to give away the beautiful thing he'd once purchased and kept in the basement of his gallery...

Nowadays, indeed, art and beauty are often difficult to connect... but I still feel that somehow they are related to each other – art is either trying to oppose beauty or deny it, but it's still somehow occupied with it...

Of course, the lack of money bothered Emil. But he considered it temporary, as always. He said that he'd always lived in debt and occasionally reduced it, and even got out of it, just like recently – in the mid-eighties.

"Det var sköna dagar..." he liked to mumble; his eyes lit up at remembering those beautiful days, and I felt that it was not so much because of the money that those days had given him, but because the whole world then had been enchanted by art, that art had conquered the market and the hearts of businessmen... beauty (or dealing with it) had become the most valued merchandise, and in Emil's opinion this was exactly how it should be – everything else, all of the goods that people had to get, whether for staying alive or facilitating life, were just means of making enjoying beauty even more pleasurable... fortunately, at the same time his notion of beauty was peculiarly broad. It included both earnest aesthetes and those who would have been offended by having their works labelled as 'beautiful'. In fact he seemed to refer to everything he considered good art as beautiful. And I think the words *skön, jätteskön, himmlaskön* contained more than a judgment on the picture in question, that they contained a plan or a dream about trading the picture... and he didn't really say much more about art or artists – he looked, selected – tasted – bought, sold... words were not needed there and he didn't even seem to value words especially. Even less did he value performances,

'performance art' – to put it more precisely – everything that is impossible to put into a depository, impossible to keep – this has no value, he said...

As for beauty, I was once painting a picture of a house, or actually a Kopli barracks building. It was just five years ago, but to me it felt really long ago – like when I was a girl, when I didn't yet know Emil but I already knew that someone very warm, and nice to press yourself against, can suddenly turn into a cold claylike shell... perhaps for that experience the whole world felt cold, grey and dank, although it wasn't like this then, although all the other Estonians, from nationalists to communists, were unanimously fighting for Estonia's independence – but I was painting this bluish-grey Kopli barracks building. Because it felt like this rotten, crooked building with its peeling paint and hanging-off front door – where people were still living – embodied the depression of the whole world... actually I couldn't even consider myself an artist yet, at least in my own opinion – I didn't know what I was doing or how I wanted to do it, I only knew that technically I could paint and draw.

I didn't put the easel in front of that building. I did take a few slides, but didn't look at those much, either, only at the very beginning... yes, I actually examined them thoroughly before I began, but later on it seemed to me that everything must be done from memory, that I have to face that mental image alone – and this is why I did it in watercolour, because a mental image is always somehow transparent... I made so many of them – this house in various lights, in different seasons... several of those pictures went wrong, of course, and simply had to be thrown away – because they lacked this something that I painted them for, something that made this house painfully ugly in my eyes and turned it into a manifestation of all this ugliness that hurt me... and when Emil later looked at those pictures, the ones I had selected and kept as pinnacles of ugliness, he called out *himmlaskön*!... these pictures sold well – or perhaps everything that could be called art sold well in those days? But for me, in addition to money this Tsarist barracks also earned me the title 'artist'... or even the sense, feeling or awareness that I knew what I wanted to express... although this sense wasn't brought about by talent as much as by this crazy perseverance – if you paint a whole exhibition full of the same building, then you will perhaps even start feeling yourself that there has to be something behind it, at least madness... in fact, this grey-blue barracks somehow came to be associated with my mother's body in my mind that mother had left behind, and maybe others noticed it in some way, maybe precisely for this endless repetition... actually, I wouldn't have wanted to sell those pictures... I'm still bothered by the feeling that in selling them I was trading something, selling piece by piece something one mustn't even offer for sale... and now I've only got a couple of them left at home! There might be some more in the basement of Emil's gallery – I'm quite certain he didn't have the heart to sell them all, but surely I won't get in there any more, and if I were to do it again now, I'd paint this building completely differently... or, in fact, not at all – once you've completed something there's no point going back to it again!

Emil was wrong to some extent, in not appreciating performance art as compared to sculpted or painted art. Because for an artist it's all the same – everything is temporary.

Baltic Belles

Because if you're worth enough or well-enough advertised, everything gets bought off you, and you have to sell if you want to make more because every tube of paint and every sheet of good paper costs a lot of money and who could hope to get as rich as Picasso in the future, to start buying back their pictures from the world! Or what would be the point of that... or actually I don't even know if he was that opposed to performance art. He just claimed sometimes that soon there would be no one who could tell what art is and if it exists at all, that it's getting more and more transient and questionable and finally altogether pointless – and then it will be gone...

Quite possibly he was right, but you shouldn't think that way if you want to make art... if you've decided to live or to make art, it's not very sensible to think about its perishability or questionability... so I thought... maybe I still think like this, although the boundaries of life have somehow become questionable – they should be clearer now, but it seems to be the other way round... have I now got back into my childhood?

When I was small I scared my mother and grandmother by following them around and complaining that I felt like I was 'in a dream'. I really didn't want to bully them, I did feel bad, as if I had some illness and as if they could help in some way... it wasn't at all like in a film or a story where one comes round after a serious illness or gets into an unbelievable situation and is then wondering – am I dreaming, or what? This feeling came over me in the middle of the most ordinary day – the feeling that I was in a dream, and that mother and grandmother, too, were part of that dream, that all this together wasn't real and that I was viewing it from somewhere else. Perhaps this was why the feeling frightened me so much – that I might suddenly wake up away from mother and grandmother and everything that should be certain... this was such an unpleasantly hazy state... as I got older it went away. Perhaps I was no longer able to perceive such an immediate feeling from the inside, as my knowledge of the world increased; I know there are all kinds of theories, and I know there might be life after death and reincarnation, and all this could be a mere illusion... all this accumulated knowledge and one's experience of life make this life seem very real – like well-worn shoes that you no longer notice on your feet... I've had so much to do with life that I've had no time to think or feel whether it's all real or not – or at least, no time to worry about it.

And yet it's no longer like that 'in a dream' feeling, not at all like that, because then reality became as if unreal and I was afraid to lose it, but now something else is pressing in and feels as real and clear like reality...

That morning I was sitting at the kitchen table, looking at the male and female caretakers trying to hoist up the flag in the street below, or in fact on the steps of the building opposite. They had carried out this routine on the morning of every flag day – the same man and woman, the flags had changed – from red to blue, black and white, but they seemed eternal. Especially the woman – she stood like a big hot loaf of white bread... or instead like a symbol of a big hot loaf of white bread, as the bread wouldn't really stand up so steadily, but this symbol seemed to belong in human life so definitely and inevitably... she was holding the flag like a halberd and the small lean stooping man was clambering around her like... who? Like a cockroach around white bread, then? In fact, he wasn't interested in his partner at that moment, but in the question of how to get the flag up into the holder beside the door. On every public holiday he had solved the question successfully, despite the colour of the flag. They had done this work in the early hours, so I had rarely been able to watch them, but now I was still breastfeeding Emilia.

To my mind this is one of the worst things about all this children stuff – giving birth and bringing them up – for months to wake up every morning as a cow: with a full, dripping udder, sticky... this is why I started to feed her from both breasts as soon as possible, so I could put the baby back down and wash myself and feel like a human not an animal with two full udders... and then to go to the kitchen, make myself a cup of strong coffee and look down at the street – like when I was still a girl, single and free... then I didn't notice that I was free – then I was attached to other things and couldn't even imagine how much a child may tie you down – as if I was no longer myself really but the means for somebody else's life...

Today, raising the flag seemed quite impossible – the wind wasn't just strong, it was completely crazy, and although the flag was neatly rolled around the pole, even like this it seemed to have decided to drag the man into the air... the caretaker flying in the wind... this variation seemed sacrilegious to me for some reason, like something you should quickly get out of your head...

But instead an energetically dreamy waltz melody started humming in my head:

The homeland hears, the homeland sees
Him flying in the winds of blue heights...

Baltic Belles

This sounded like a double blasphemy: firstly, this Stalinist dream did not match with our blue-black-white in the least; secondly, my father would certainly not have accepted the Red Eagle of one of his favourite songs being replaced with a caretaker. And neither party would care for my explanation that such associations appear in my mind in an instant and of their own accord... or is all this perhaps the bad influence of Chagall? He too had people in boots floating up in the sky, after all? Nowadays if that is the moment you get an interesting thought you might as well start guessing whose influence is manifesting itself in it, because surely someone somewhere has already thought something similar...

I remember that I also racked my brains over who in Sweden puts out flags in the morning. I had never before thought of it. Caretakers, I guess, but probably migrant workers – immigrants – some Turk, Somalian or Estonian... certainly not such an old man, well into retirement age... but they too equally certainly, are not locals – just looking from the window upstairs it is clear that they can't speak the state language, and I don't suppose they've been granted citizenship for achievements of special merit... what should one call them? Resident occupants, perhaps?... they probably don't rack their brains over this themselves, surely they're just happy that they're allowed to carry on pottering around here and not forced into retirement – for on a pension you can't eat so well that you look like a warm loaf... and surely they're putting up this flag just as dutifully as the previous one – this action doesn't require any knowledge of the state language.

Finally they got the flag up. I don't remember how exactly. I must've been looking at something else for a while – perhaps the sky, where layers of clouds were storming past at varied speeds; at times the lower – the darker, stormier ones – cast down rain, like bursts of crying... then I noticed the flag was flying half-mast, and immediately thought, who knows why, that well, that must be Meri – as there isn't any anniversary of any deportations today, but for the President they'd put a flag up, I suppose, and based on his appearance they should have black ribbons at hand at all times – so wobbly and thin, like he should be protected from a stronger gale, although in fact he was rather tough – like Estonian stubbornness... and is he really gone now?

But the association for some reason was completely different, it had nothing to do with the president or any other person – from somewhere a phrase popped out: *Meri andis, meri võttis* – the sea gave and the sea took... or not really 'from somewhere' – of course the phrase popped up only because it was the only saying I knew about the sea... a really tired saying, too. But for some reason it started repeating itself in my head, again and again: the sea gave – the sea took... the sea gave – the sea took...

And then someone behind me said, *"Estonia pogibla!"*

I turned round and jumped up quickly, almost knocking over the chair, because for a moment I didn't understand a thing – I guess I'd always thought that when such a thing is said in Russian, it is said with *schadenfreude*, but now the one saying it was Mrs Valia, Mrs Valia next door, and even though she was Russian, she would hardly take pleasure in the destruction of Estonia and hurry to announce it to me: my father might have been militaristic but she was broad-minded, perhaps even with a sense of guilt; but then I saw that there was no *schadenfreude* in her, that she was crying instead, and I asked, still completely perplexed: *"Kak – pogibla?"*

Because how could Estonia suddenly be destroyed without me having a clue about it?

"Utonula!" she said, *"Sovsem utonula!"*

Then I realised that it was the ship, *Estonia*, that operated on the line to Sweden, that I had almost pushed Emil onto the previous evening. But actually I still couldn't understand a thing because I had taken that ship myself, across a pretty heavy sea, and it had felt really large and dependable, much more dependable than our little state that Russian tanks can run over again, whenever they feel like it… and then suddenly I realised completely – that Emil may have got wet and he might be cold!

That if Estonia has indeed completely sunk, Emil might be flapping in some lifeboat, with waves constantly washing over, and he might be cold – and this didn't suit him at all, because he hated damp and cold – this was actually the only thing he couldn't accept here in Estonia, that our rooms were cold and damp like cellars, that it was not only impossible to live here, but also to think… but Valia stared at me blankly, as if looking into an open grave.

"Oh, dear child, dear child!" she repeated, put her arms around me and burst into tears again.

2000

Translated by Eva Finch and Jason Finch

The Bolide Shard
Asta Põldmäe

1

In late summer, after the bolide flew over, appeals for shards from it turned up in the papers. Several observers had noticed that in the northeast, quite near the horizon, the luminous body had suddenly burst, sending out rays, which slowed down a bit and continued their journey in the same direction at different speeds. Some said that while it seemed to be nearby, the meteorite shower might actually have hit southern Finland or even southeastern Sweden.

The summer was blazing away the last hours before its death and it was difficult to think of its black evenings as belonging together with the glistening white, still tranquil days of high summer. Days still long and striped with swallows. And so there was enough light to notice anything, particularly if a star that had been blown to pieces was lying somewhere!

Ernst did not find a thing, although this year he was running late moving out of their summerhouse. More than once he had to walk there from the railway station, both with or without luggage, covering the lonely roads through forests and crops. But he didn't even look down much. Anyway, who says it's lonely places in particular that a meteorite shard seeks? If you came from an utterly lonely place perhaps you'd prefer to land

Baltic Belles

in the heart of the action...

Ernst had some such thoughts, anyway, and he kept his eyes peeled when he happened to remember to do that. Moreover, he tended to find stuff without looking for it: wrist bags and car keys, glasses, mobile phones, gloves, and once even a small child who spoke Russian. This brought him quite a bit of trouble with the police when he tried to get the child back to where he belonged. The child, in its underwear and blue woollen socks, toddled in front of him on Taara Boulevard, when a green city bus, heavy and smoking, slid past on the other side of the sparse row of oaks. What would have happened if the child had made a careless sideways step...? Ernst had picked the child up, and he tried to hand him over in the shop; the women who work in the small grocery shop at this end of Tähtvere see the people of their street with children and dogs day after day, year after year. But no, this child was not known to them. Should he call the police? Then he'd have to stay put until the emergency vehicle arrived, which might not happen that quickly. In a stuffy butcher's shop with a full briefcase and a toddler! No, he felt he'd rather take the little boy home and then make a phone call; the corner of Koidula Street, on which his house stood, was really just a small distance away.

In the course of this short journey it occurred to him that this child might easily stay with him! If no one came along, if nothing got figured out, if there seemed to be too much paperwork... the little boy of two or so who had just started to walk, who didn't (or couldn't) say his name, but from out of whose sporadic babbling Russian words could be heard. The child was not scared, and, strangely enough, was not crying, either. The little bean-shaped stone, which he refused to put down, as if it were a talisman, he knew to be an elf's foot.

They had eaten more than once, the child had even had a nap, when towards the evening, in the twilight, the young mother arrived.

Irritated, breathless from running round, she came in almost without knocking, quickly hit the child three or four times, stopped for a moment as if wondering whether she should hit Ernst too, and left without thanking him, without saying a word, running, like she'd come, the child under her arm, long legs flashing under the denim skirt, and without looking back, down the stairs.

Of course, Ernst was used to this. He had exceptional eyesight. The ground was always too littered, there was nothing much to look at and discoveries brought constant hassle, but what could he do? If you've had good fortune, you can't get smug about it.

Also, how much of it had been up to him, anyway, this evening when he had been the only one to get off and, at the barley field at Tõravere station, where suddenly it clearly smelled of warm barley bread? Where would have been a better place for it to have landed, such as southeastern Sweden? Tõravere observatory with its patented neutrino, the whole building full of qualified astronomers – is that not enough? And the terra-stucco-grey main building was just tall enough to look out over the elevated land. In the depths of August serenity, in the tepidity of summer evening that wants to know nothing.

In the midst of some whitish, slightly flattened grain a brown patch, almost pitch black in the centre, could be seen. The soil at the edges of the crater was hemmed in by a delicate frost-like fuzz. Quietly, like an egg in the nest, a shard of the bolide was gleaming in the bottom of the pit. It was roughly the size of a fur hat, hissing, smoking, and, of course, terribly hot. Ernst glanced back towards the railway – in the bluish wetland mist the back of the rear engine of the departing Elva-Tartu train was disappearing among the alders. Gone.

No person was about, although a flock of jackdaws had settled down in the vetch nearby. The sky above the hill remained lifelessly bone-coloured. Above the hill the domes of the observatory were shining like three sleeping bald heads. It was a Sunday with its incubatory sunset.

In such a place, on such an evening, even those who aren't sleeping are asleep. They are imitating wakefulness, unsuccessfully. These summer evening Estonian village streets with their closed half-curtains of floral calico, as if with writing on them: *Do not disturb; outside is nothing to do with us*. Ernst did have a mobile phone, but who would he call? The fire station? There was no fire. The little piece of a star sitting in the earthy crater, even if hot, did not pose a direct danger. The rescue service? The weather station? Who is responsible for fallen stars on Sunday evenings? Of course, the finder should take the shard up the hill, to the observatory. Or to the Institute of Geology? Or directly to Anto Raukas? But aren't people and institutions like that chiefly interested in cooled-down consignments from outer space? Even more if it's properly underground, occupying earth on top of it and millennia in its biography. Where would he, Ernst, get those millennia from? Moreover, it was the holidays for academics. He could have done with some fire tongs, in any case!

The choice remained: to sit in the barley field all night

long, preventing – how? – the barley from catching fire (what need for those constantly smouldering Australias or Beyond-Moscows here in the spruce grove of Vapramäe?) or, despite it all, to work out some way of getting the celestial stone home. A new brass fireguard, seventy by seventy had just been nailed onto the floor. In that respect, yes! He could wet the floor, put damp sheets around it. A spark fears water like fire, and it can't be that different with a star.

Oh, the childishness of it! Ernst was, it seemed, more of a scientist than he would have suspected. It could be different with a star. It must be very different with a star.

The barley did seem, probably due to the heated soil, a bit browner at the edges of the crater, as if ashamed of its single year of life compared to the other one's light years, making an effort to look older and more mature within its brief span. At times, it seemed to Ernst that the crop was already getting scorched a bit. A light breeze was brushing across the field just now. The train he'd come down on was hooting on its return journey. Three quarters of an hour had gone in the blink of an eye. Gone like a human life among geological eras.

Ernst set off running down the slope. The growing barley was replaced by sparse stacks of early-harvested rye. That rye was still tied up and set in stacks! The strip of land was probably too steep, too narrow and ran down to a stream – they didn't dare bring heavy machinery here, for obvious reasons. Signs of departing summer, as well as departing time.

He hurried through the mixed pine grove to the summerhouse. There he wrapped birch bark around the handle of an enamelled bucket, wondering whether to lay a piece of wet sacking in the bottom, but a deep-down sense of decency

Baltic Belles

ruled out such crude means. Fire tongs and canvas workgloves in his other hand, he was already out of the gate, when he turned back, the blood ticking anxiously in his ears like an infernal machine at work. He scraped three dustpanfuls of ashes out of the fireplace, to make bedding for the piece of star, as if it was a living creature, some unpredictable fairy of the hearth, for whom he now had to make a home, and – now downstairs – squeezed the heavy wooden lid of the jam cauldron into the bucket as a cover. The protruding prong of his rucksack's buckle got tangled in the strap of a floral-patterned apron thrown onto the hook, pulling Ernst back for a moment. A tug, and he was gone.

In the field of low grain, quickly sinking into the darkness of an August night, a white thread of smoke was rising straight into the sky. Silently, as if from a sacrificial brazier. The star was still there, glistening darkly, greasily, the lump blinked bluish in the twilight. The fading and brightening rhythm of the glow, which, pulsating, exposed the pale lightness of the circle of stalks and hid them again – it was like a breathing human chest. The field seemed alive, too. Ernst would not have been surprised if the land had stirred under the soles of his baseball boots. Like a sleeper does, starting for no reason, trying to find a more comfortable position for his shoulders.

Ernst lay down next to the crater, resting his chin on his hand. It smelled metallic, like welding smells – is that what the welded seam of the starry sky and the horizon would smell like, if only someone could get there and inhale? Somehow this seam had now ripped open, the spotted lid had opened a bit. Something immeasurable, unachievable for an earthly human being was suddenly at his feet like a tiny abandoned bundle.

He pulled on the canvas gloves.

"No need to make an issue of it, although you are definitely accustomed to different ways," he explained to the star, to buy some time, for some reason addressing the visitor formally and half-whispering, but then forgetting to whisper and speaking aloud, while jumping up and hoisting the star aloft in the fire tongs. "Don't worry, we've got reasonable conditions. Of course, I fully understand your confusion: a dented pail for salting mushrooms is no good, quite right, if one has come that far, but there wasn't any other iron thing to hand in the house..."

For a moment, the star almost slipped out of his grasp, but Ernst squeezed the tongs and grasped the edge of the bucket under the lump. There would have been the plastic berry-picking bucket, bigger than this one, yellow. Its handle comes off, though it's some cheap Salvo thing... yes, and who says its bottom wouldn't melt off in the process?

Ernst was considering whether to go back to the summerhouse and bring the empty birdcage from the shed, from which the green parrot had flown away. He now covered the bucket with the fire blanket... when it suddenly seemed to him that the star moved. In one of its grooves, or even two of them, something flashed.

Darkly.

Deeply.

Surrounded by dense needles of fire like long eyelashes.

But what was not radiating here! Instead of going out, the lump seemed to heat up more. Now some of its matt sides without any visible glow were also pulsating. The grain around them was undulating to its rhythm. The large face of the moon dragged itself above the tree tops of the forest, a distant smile on the petrified baby cheeks.

"And take, for instance, these tongs." Was Ernst trying to muffle his growing uneasiness by speaking? "These tongs are also for moving all sorts of nasty things, such as a smouldering firebrand, a blocked ash griddle or rotten potatoes at the bottom of the crate, while you as a star…"

With sufficient aloofness, the star freed itself with a slight, impatient shake, almost a shrug, from the grip of the grimy tongs and slid into the bucket of its own accord.

It did not like the ash. A snort, grumpy and astonished, made this clear. It may even have been a sneeze. To turn up with your ash somewhere, where for eons there's been nothing but gleaming going on! But some insulation was necessary. Even this way the hot side of the bucket was burning his leg through his thin poplin summer trousers. Burning like hell. Good thing he'd put the canvas gloves on! And when the Valga-Tartu night train rolled in, slowed down and dropped off a dopey-looking, unsteady man in a crumpled linen suit – even from behind Ernst could have sworn that it was the writer Kabur, if that polyglot hadn't been resting in the sand of Metsakalmistu cemetery for years now – and then Ernst, desperately grabbing hold of the hot bucket, jumped onto the bottom step of the last carriage and managed to heave himself onto the train, which was already gaining speed.

2

In Ernst's shabby researcher's flat, last properly renovated long ago, the same flat with its broken wood-heated boiler which had almost gassed him last winter, he was – or should we say they were? – welcomed by deep midnight silence. A note was lying below the coat rack. Ethel? Had she been here? Had she perhaps come back?

No, she hadn't come back. Several long seconds passed before Ernst realised that this too, was his own note. His letter to himself. Such self-deception was, of course, childish, but nothing is to be condemned as pathetic, if the jaws of silence – night silence, day silence, Midsummer night silence, Christmas Eve silence, Sunday silence, tired silence and rested silence, all the silences – have closed over you.

After Ethel had carried her suitcases into the taxi one day – now long ago – even waving from the car door, smiling, as if hurrying off on another last-minute Southern holiday, just not saying this time how long she'd be away or where she was going, after this she hadn't come back. Not said anything, either. Ernst, however – he, apparently, had to be clever enough to know where the taxi had taken her. He didn't.

So, Ernst had started to leave notes under the coat rack when he was going out, just like they used to do between them. Just like they do in many homes. So that he could believe, in the course of those five or six steps from the door to the coat rack – that this one wasn't his own one. It was.

It was. And this strange, dense nocturnal silence meeting him at the door was also his own. Like oxygenated air, which you breathe through the mask until your head starts humming and gets light, while a huge dark void grows inside your chest. There had been such an enormous silence in their home the whole time he was writing the dissertation, that their flat wasn't big enough to hold it. Where could it fit itself, where could it hide, when Ernst came back from giving an evening lecture, from an expedition, a late flight or even the summerhouse in Tõravere, where Ethel hadn't been for a long time and wasn't going to go any more? Where could such an enormous lump of silence hide, so as to collapse on top of the person coming in the door – an eyeless canvas of sky falling onto the small unsuspecting human?

It wasn't an eyeless canvas that had fallen onto Ernst that August night when he had returned from getting their summer home ready for winter, but the fiery eye of this canopy. The newcomer had to be welcomed, it couldn't be left in that sorry bucket just gobbling up ashes. The bath? No, that would be just as disrespectful as the wet piece of sacking. Cellar? Well, no. In summer, the cellar belonged to the vagabond. Old Mitt, hairy, knocking with the stick, politely squeezing the broken portable radio fixed with tape against his ear; old Mitt, who did have a home, a family even, but in addition to those treasures a measureless desire to wander around. If one just left the cellar windows open in hot weather to dry the fire wood, no force could stop the old man from climbing in.

3

Appointed to follow one's star, one should reach out for the heavens. What was Ernst now to do? Fall face down onto the earth? Was it his star in the first place, and not just a random one? Who had chosen it for him and did he deserve it? He had this exceptional vision, after all; he was a finder; chance selected him, not the other way round! Did this count for anything? Why had he pursued writing his dissertation these four long years, paying for it by losing Ethel? He had dreamed of a star and yet he'd been sent a piece of a star, a vague shard, the nature, mood and hazards of which he couldn't even imagine. Did this mean that he was the chosen one? Or was it merely that destiny had decided to play a practical joke on him?

Ernst had virtually no place to put his unusual find. So what was he supposed to do with an unextinguished star in his flammable realm? *Herbarium Cladoniae Estonici* – that was the fancy name the room had where Ernst had, since his years of study, gathered more or less all of the Estonian varieties of lichen. Every wall and drawer was full of moss in envelopes, frames, bunches and boxes; they were hanging from rails suspended below the ceiling, on the washing line. The whole flat was literally filled with the scent of the dissertation. The canvas hat hanging on the hook, the worthy parka jacket almost entirely consisting of pockets, the same one that Ethel had lovingly washed and ironed in the early years, more than once mended with needle and thread. Even more often than necessary. This was when bells were ringing and they had fed each other with spoons. Acting with joy was like acting with increased strength – who, who could measure the power of joy! Until the jacket became a forgotten rag, which wouldn't even fit in the washing machine...

But the work at the university went on smoothly: his enthusiasm was intoxicating and his bones seemed to be singing in his body. His field of study was absolutely spot-on. There is never much time to look down from the flying carpet of rapture.

Ernst's research quickly earned international attention;

Baltic Belles

invitations to conferences and expeditions were flooding in; now he was teaching specialisation courses, supervising postgraduate students, sending off the chapters of his dissertation for publication. Not only the morning hour, which was indeed passing, but the whole day arching before him seemed to carry gold with it.

The pouch of samples attached to his belt was always expanding. With his wide-legged boots on and his inseparable knife in hand, he had burrowed through both the moss covering of his familiar rocks as well as all of the patches of land which were of any geobotanical interest. The thesis had filled three volumes and threatened to reach a fourth. Few botanists manage to discover new species, but by now there were more than thirty in Ernst's name. This small old country was frightfully mossy!

On the floor in front of the stove the seventy by seventy sheet of brass was shining yellow. This is where Ernst carefully slid his guest down the side of the bucket.

In a short restless sleep Ernst was standing on the open hatch of the hayloft, defending the entrance from the attacking uproar of sparks, a wet piece of sacking in his hand. As far as the horizon everything was roaring in flames. The loft behind him was filled with lichen instead of hay.

When he woke in the morning, the star was almost in its original position, at the corner of the window near the fireguard, but it had moved to turn its rough side against the floor, while its rounded and smooth side, as if shaped by a wet palm, was looking upward. Yes, in daylight maturely brown and probably no longer even hot, it looked like a loaf of bread that had come out of the oven and was cooling. Egg on top, pork on the bottom! Ethel, the little city woman, had never shaped such things, but Ernst's mother with her home economy training had. "Bread that looks like stone," Ernst could not help thinking. "Or bread in place of the stone? Or stone at night and bread in the day?" And just like with the child he once found in Taara Boulevard, the thought slipped through his mind that the star might – who knows under what circumstances, now it was entirely up to him, after all! – that the star might stay with him.

But there was no escape from the need to get some real bread; in the cupboard there was only a tin of sardines and a couple of dry garlic cloves. Should the star go into the cold oven in the meantime? Or the fridge? The shard seemed lifeless, or was it asleep... Ernst was not yet familiar with its ways. However, the lump was too heavy to be taken along to the shop.

Ernst gently lay the fire blanket over the star.

He ran the whole way.

With horrifying mental images of flames bursting out of the windows, firemen crowding the tiny wedge-shaped yard of the pre-war Tähtvere house, his tension abated in the sincere brightness of the summer's day. The halogen-white business-like air of the big supermarket embodied a quite different, mercantile world. 'Mummy kills us if we don't eat our soup!' – a group of jolly youths, euphorically certain of the eternal survival of their home, cried out from a brown and white poster. These were beautiful children from good homes, in designer label clothes and on expensive bicycles. They were cared for; their parents' unconditional love was their trump card, their capital. They had something to boast of. It pulled at the heart as if with thin red thread.

"Cats would buy this!" a plump Mongol-cheeked cat insisted in another poster. Every anxiety simply had to feel like an exaggeration here. The bromelias of the flower stand had eaten flesh and drunk blood. Bigger-than-lifesize roses were panting. To carry a soul even deep within and invisible here meant blaspheming the god of the marketplace and ridiculing oneself. "Vulgarity is like a tombstone through which no voice reaches the deceased," Ernst remembered Mauriac's words and right then felt ashamed of his dirty mind. As if anybody had forced him to come here: he had come voluntarily. He had come for real bread.

"You can give me the list, I'll weigh stuff for you," said Ly obligingly, reaching out her hand over the counter to Ernst. A prompt excuse was now needed so Ernst could politely decline this kind offer made by his classmate: "Thanks. Ethel forgot to give me the order, today I have to know myself."

But noticing the other's face brightening up with understanding and hearing her bursting out laughing Ernst realised that there was no point going on lying, and thought it better to hear what Ly had to say.

"Silly me," Ly mocked, with a bit of flirtation. "Can't remember a thing. Your Ethel has travelled to Caracas, hasn't she? The postcard was all full of Venezuelan stamps with crocs. Good thing it hadn't been nicked from the post box. Once a letter from Australia went the same way: my cousin inquired, but I hadn't even seen the letter."

Caracas! No trip lasts for two and a half months.

He himself had been the one in the family who had

apathetically put off any discussion, unwilling to question Ethel's right to make her own decisions. Unwilling to set up barriers against that gentle yet internally smouldering nature of hers. And what had he had to offer to Ethel all these years he had been writing the thesis? Those years in which travelling had become a pandemic around them. They had not had children during those seven shared years, so there was nothing to stop them in that respect. But he had been sitting in his laboratories, endlessly checking the primary data, repeating and rechecking the geobotanical analyses, turning down invitations, outings, the simplest garden party. Until he and Ethel were no longer invited.

Ernst did not want to call the cartoon dubbing studio, where Ethel with her fluent English and Spanish had been working, and perhaps still was. "Bright and good with her hands, of course she will manage, sure she will. Could train to be a cook," Ernst mused with a sad smile. The whole world was training to be cooks. Who knew how many Estonian women, this very moment, were drawing tiramisu hearts onto the golden dessert plate of some oil tycoon. Oh! Whether irony or self-irony – both of these failed to be reassuring right now.

Quickly, without looking, Ernst threw cool flat packets of meat and salami slices into the basket. The good thing about having no family is that you don't have to cook: he had repeated his mother's wisdom to himself. Although his mother had always cared for Ethel, her warm simplicity – with her rough truth she had quietly been nudging the daughter-in-law out of her son's imaginary inner circle. Just in case. With some instinct of a mother of sons, preparing him for less hurt. Until the time arrived to find support from the bitter goodness of maternal wisdom.

The sale was in full swing. Pink sheets of plastic wrapped around the boxes of goods were glistening with shameless indiscretion; through the loudspeakers they recommended some wonderful nail varnish, invited you to find money coupons in packets of Laima marshmallows. Deafened by the noise, Ernst grabbed his shopping items from their usual places without looking at their prices and hurried towards the checkouts, when suddenly a temporary stall blocking the aisle, behind which an old woman offered dips to sample, suddenly attracted his attention. On the bench beside it, playing with a red glossy plastic glasses' case, making the buzzing sound of a car engine, lips puckered, was none other than the Russian-speaking little boy, who once had spent half a day with him. The same sticking-up brown hair, round eyes, the pleasantly smiley lower lip. It was probably the boy's grandmother selling the dips here.

Ernst inadvertently stopped to watch the child. The lack of wheels didn't bother the toddler. The grandmother's worried glance every now and then fell on the child, while her thin hands, covered in capillaries, quickly stuck strips of bread into the dip, reaching the plate out to passers-by.

In the shopping commotion no one much wanted to taste or purchase the dip, and the old woman, seeing Ernst's regarding the little boy, said with a sigh, "It's not good form these days for a grown man to watch a child he doesn't know. Off you go, sir."

And then as if startled, remembering that the shop manager had particularly pointed this out to her, a temporary worker: the obligation to be as pleasant as possible to the customers, she said apologetically, "Unless you would like to buy a dip, sir."

But treating potential customers in such an openly self-serving way was probably also unacceptable.

And this man here clearly wasn't interested...

The old woman peeped around her, perplexed, keeping an eye on the little boy at all times: don't let the manager hear how she dares to reprimand a customer, now!

But to her surprise, the stranger suddenly said warmly: "The little fellow and I are no strangers. We know each other."

"Where do you know him from?"

"The little chap was left with me for half a day."

"What do you mean, left with you?" the woman said, confused. "Dima has a place at Tarmeko kindergarten and he spends his days there." And, having considered it and hesitated for a moment, added with folksy ingenuousness, "Yelizaveta did of course have some boyfriends, but you I haven't seen. Leave the child alone. None of those so-called fathers have taken any interest in the child so far. And now the mother doesn't any more, either."

"I once found this child at Taara Boulevard, in his underwear. He could've wandered in front of a bus. I took him home with me."

"Very nice."

But Ernst was not troubled by her harsh tone of voice. He continued, "It was nice, actually. The little fellow slept, then ate a bit. Didn't say a word. Ate again. Slept again. We never had a chat. And in the evening the worried young mother came running in."

"This worried young mother," the old woman's voice was bitter, mocking, "Liisa, my daughter, should've stayed with you that time. Can't tell a proper man, runs around, tail up..."

"Madam," Ernst now had to explain, "how could your daughter have stayed with me if we didn't know each other at all?"

Moreover, this young woman had hit the child and considered whether to also hit him, Ernst.

But the old woman said with sudden decisiveness, "Now she has gone to Turkey to do belly dancing. To be a hooker."

Ernst remembered the star.

Having hurriedly given Alexandra Dunayeva his phone number and a request to definitely call in with Dima some time, Ernst hurried home. If one studied the law, one might be able to think of a way to secure the little boy's life in this world where he so early has found himself, the thread supporting him too fragile. Home, where everything was hanging on by an even thinner thread.

Had he not left his home in the powers of the force completely unknown for too long! "Turkey!" he thought to himself, perplexed, walking quickly along the broken pavement. "Turkey! Caracas!" And then immediately felt guilty for putting those two place names together, as if even such a combination was hiding something obscene. "Turkey!" As if the earth had run out of places!

Had the whole universe run out of room, so that now a star had flown from outer space to him, Ernst Lambert?

4

Out of his habit of keeping field-trip journals and, lately, to just verbalise his lonely thoughts for himself, Ernst Lambert had gathered a few notes about the current phase of his life.

***

The star staying with me in my home changed everything.

Up till then I had willingly stayed in the laboratory till late at night, would have even stayed till the morning.

A night person is something quite different from a day person. I didn't want to meet what I was at night.

At home.

In my empty home.

And you always found things to do in the lab.

Now, strangely enough, I felt like hurrying home. First it was easy to rationalise: the piece of star doesn't deserve to be trusted! And I've got my lichen at home. Ethel might be back! A letter may have arrived! Whatever...

No, all this wasn't true. Little wings had started to grow on my heels and these were not from any earthly material.

My home was no longer such a lifeless den with its cold kitchen, its ugly gas cylinder, its forgotten musty corners. The air of this home had ceased to be sad. The unpleasant dwelling with its worn rust coloured sofas got filled with lightness, motion, sudden flashes. Rustles and echoes lived there, which I had never met in the stuffy cramped flat. Even the eerie gleam of the guts of the fridge now glowed like a friendly hearth, in which tomatoes ripened and rock-hard tasteless avocados got butter-yellow tasty flesh. A new defining factor had started to bend the most basic conditions of my existence. You couldn't see this defining factor, but it could be felt everywhere.

Baltic Belles

How many sparks, how many tiny ephemeral stars one single star can give! Playfully, multiplicity had entered my lonely life and opened its palm.

Having for years been fond of lichens, those children grown prematurely old on northern slopes, I had forgotten that light, only light does everything. I had forgotten how a hard whitewashed ceiling, a partition hiding shabbiness, a neglected human chest can meet rays of light. With a cheer, the southern sun penetrated the dank rooms on the northern side, where it had never been before. It forgot to leave even on cloudy days, even in the evening, and I had to find explanations for the neighbours why my windows were filled with dazzling light late into the night, while in the whole Tähtvere district and above the river, always light on windless nights, the sky stayed still, ink black.

It had many modes. The star could gather itself together, be narrow like a sling, then again flood rumbustiously with zest for life. One moment diffuse like mist, it could quickly intensify into glassy pitch-black obsidian, congealed lava stone, the sort that sleeps on the slopes of dormant volcanos. I no longer wanted to sleep, and nor did it: my closed eyelids were pricked with painful needles. I wanted nothing but for it to burn to the end and then fall into it. Everything was happiness. Everything was creation.

It became restless when I had to leave home and hid when I returned, to get its own back on me. My love increased its size while my neglect decreased it. More sinuous than longing, it was unbelievably tough at the same time. When I embraced it, it slimmed down and became more supple, the way no earthly woman can, and all of a sudden this tall slenderness burst into a spiralling fan-like flood, which fell down onto the earth like a rain of sparks. Or it darted straight into the sky right before my eyes, somewhere I never thought it could reach, as it wasn't a star but just a fallen shard. But it too, like everything created as earthly, had an integrity that was given by love, and thus I could not be sure of anything. I couldn't be sure that one day, one night it wouldn't be flying in the sky again with all its sisters. 'To Turkey,' I sneered aloud in my sullen moments of insecurity, full of the familiar anticipation of being abandoned. 'To Turkey,' the echoes repeated in the corners, accompanied by a weak rustling sound.

However, no time was given for the fear to penetrate, before it again carried me along, again and again. I became radiance, timelessness, peace, happy peace, with nothing to pursue. Completely exhausted, I fell asleep, head on the communion table of its belly, while it was thoughtfully awake. Its eyes, two motionless lakes of obsidian, were shimmering gently, and in those moments I didn't believe time existed when I stopped sinking into those lakes.

I couldn't talk to my friend and this troubled me, but its moods were clearly distinguishable in its untranslatable language, just as within elaborate fireworks one can distinguish roses, palms, waterfalls, swords and arrows in its fire. The spikes and falls of its moods were large-scale like the Grand Canyon, destructive like a cyclone. My research was taking place in the corner, in the form of a tall mound of papers with scorched edges, sheets curling, and none of them any longer even existing. It was a miracle that all this paper had not yet gone up in flames. And I didn't give a damn.

We played with the moss collections, threw them at each

other, frolicking and laughing. Irresponsibly, we pulled out the freshest, still moist-smelling velvety preparations. We shoved the moss into every part of each other, in games the symbolism of which I prefer to remain silent about. When people love, they do anything, and it's beautiful, but then the beauty withers and fades.

When we got tired of our frenzy, the mosses became our bed. It was nothing for light-years to lay down with geological eras, rigidity lost its boundaries with softness, absence of matter with matter – our duplicity had been proved and what else mattered?

It goes without saying that nothing was more irrelevant or secondary in this conflagration than my dissertation, that brainchild promising a glorious future, which I had put at the absolute centre of my whole life up till then. Now I was interested in another centre, in live celestial fire. This lace of lightnings, shimmering and sublime in its endless change had occupied the whole of my limited human sky and I was losing myself.

I was suffocating, but it was blissful, just like prolonged death by drowning. When I had sunk into half-consciousness, when my heartbeats were fading like the ringing of a distant bell, brought episodically to your ears by wind, only then did its snake-like grip slacken. Its regret was long, full of tenderness; it pleaded with me tearfully in its own language, but it was too late. The flash had already gone through me. I had looked into the bottom of the gorge and tasted the heavenly flavour of returning to life.

No one was supposed to see my fear of death, but now someone had seen it. I felt humiliated. Yet I loved it. A year passed this way. Languageless, but not entirely, it occasionally found words for someone. On the days of its anger I made fire in the stove, which soothed the whirlwind of its rage. Particularly this last, fading blue flame above the coals a moment before closing the damper. Then it happened, that the hearth was suddenly filled with salamanders; they started their ugly unambiguous dance, in which my friend promptly joined. I assure you, those poses, this self-abandonment was unbearable to look at; their conspiracy, their nasty secret language was perfect. Just like the betrayal excluding me. I was distraught and appalled. My hours of cowering in front of the glass door of the stove – that suffering was beyond human comprehension.

I realised that I was losing her. Her sensitivity, as well as her irritation, broke out in waves, and their manifestation as power cuts was the most embarrassing aspect of it. When the cables filled with her hysteria with such tension that the fuses melted, the house fell in darkness. Then the upstairs neighbours, the professor or his wife, came to borrow candles, having no clue what the matter was. And I always had the candles at hand, long household candles, in the drawer of the shoe cupboard, the front door side.

Something in her star life was clearly incomplete and lacking. Just like in my life. In the hours of vexation she thinned and, swaying, almost bodyless, she managed to slide herself out of the chimney with the smoke, into the park. But flying in frustration, this is not like flying on the wings of ecstasy. The star got stuck in the top of the first slender lime tree and moaned there cursing for the whole night. This ancient lime tree howls and squeaks only in a November storm, not on a summer night, and I had to get a man I knew with a Pekkaniska hoist first thing in the morning. Fortunately, I knew a man like that. Because what would I have had to write on the formal order form? I need a hoist to release a star stuck in the tree by its rays? An angry star!

It became increasingly clear that she was not that wordless after all. That she simply keeps both her chattiness and the meaningfulness of her silence for someone else. It only took Dima and his grandmother, who had indeed attained the position of shop assistant in the department of ice cream and soft drinks, walking past the window, when my friend perked up, insisted that I call Dima and Alexandra Dunayeva in, and the little boy's mixed-language 'ice cream hochesh?' was the profound opening note of their meaningful dialogue. They whispered, they laughed, they had plenty of words and much wordlessness. They had plenty of games and a babbling cosiness. There somewhere, in her high freezing emptiness, my friend hadn't known to miss the warm softness of a child's palms. Now she knew about it. This had foreseeable consequences. She pulled herself together, shrank until she was as tiny as a pin cushion, like a velvety ring case; its shine softened, became deep and matt. The little boy, who now dropped in every now and then, was soon at home in their house, so that the caring wife of the professor upstairs knitted a close-fitting light blue lambswool hat for him, a small blue helmet with a warm lining.

As they chatted to each other in a language only comprehensible to the two of them, Dima was allowed to take the piece of star into the garden. He could play quietly between the woodpiles, disturbing nobody with what remained from my friend after decreasing and calming down. Only very seldom did a shard absent-mindedly glittering in the surrounding velvetiness happen to break the sun's rays so that they brightly shone into the windowpanes, and then it happened that one of the windows upstairs was pushed open and the whole weightiness of the professor's authority was heard:

"What the hell? Again that little Russian lad is playing around with fire in the garden!"

But when there was no smoke visible and things did not develop into a fire, the scholar, in creative self-abandonment, again delved into the manuscript of his monograph. 'A farm hand must eat, be the house on fire,' was the dry statement, with which he had managed to defend the fortress of his labour of the mind throughout life. And still did.

I started to see my friends more often again, but in the new term I wasn't voted back into the position of docent. My boss had shamelessly voted for someone else in the council. I, who had been forgotten because of my many absences, had been given only a quarter of my usual allocation of lectures; they had taken away the palm tree from my office and replaced it with a fig; my desk had disappeared and in its place there was a small high-gloss drawerless table from the corridor, which had previously been used for the newspapers and the water dispenser. The date for me to defend my thesis was no longer renewed.

The manuscript of my thesis, that scorched heap of papers, perhaps wasn't in such a terrible state and I probably would've been able to replace the missing pages, but I wasn't even sure I still wanted to. Calls for papers were being sent to others now; science journals stopped asking me for articles. The department secretary had forgotten to add my lectures to the curriculum and to enter them in the computer, but the protocol had already been stamped, signed by the rector, and I had to write my meagre contribution on the timetable by hand. The truncated timetable hung in the stairwell of the main building for the whole term.

I didn't have many friends but my problems had not reduced their thin ranks. In Tartu, on the contrary, one can make more friends on such an occasion. They were still ready to have a beer with me, less often someone popped in, and who could I have invited anyway... although I had more time for friends than I used to.

The backroom was now locked most of the time from the inside. My lodger was almost always asleep these days. Its fading mind found relief from something in sleep. The rare poker evenings I allowed myself in the club reduced the temperature at home almost down to freezing point; when I got back late at night, grey stars of frost were glittering on the frame of the front door of my flat. Beautiful were the days when Mehis came up from Emajõe Street.

There is nobody lighter on their feet, which were like a part of his lively imagination. His feet never got tired, he had Hermes' sandals.

Casually, just like some young Schiller, my companion of several expeditions hiked along green landscapes; he knew paths and bog islands, rides and boardwalks; he didn't count asphalt as anything. But above all he was inspired by the damp and grassy footpaths beside the railway embankment. Walking together along the path beside the railway between Peedu and Elva, sometimes even up to Tartu, he had gradually become 'mi hermano del alma' – *my soul brother.*

It was always good to sit with Mehis: even without speaking. It turned out that the language of this silence was also known to my lodger. The way the two of them conversed in silence would have made every communication guru envious. One evening, when Mehis speechlessly – as a tactful person he didn't want to bother me as I already knew the story – told my friend about his life in the chimney of the puppet museum, the look in the eyes of the star became more dense until it was dark blue and material like the Sicilian night, and she started to glitter phosphorescently, throwing shards of light off its surface in every direction. Mehis rubbed his cheek thoughtfully, still under the spell of the story. He briefly blew onto his arm, uncovered by his summer shirt, as if chasing away some nocturnal bug, said goodbye in a friendly way and left.

My lodger was furious that I had seen her shame. She raved, yelled and wept, rolled on the floor, recklessly dispersing large, daisy-sized sparks of static electricity – and I'm not exaggerating by saying that never before had my home been as close to being set on fire. I definitively started to fear and hate her.

5

This is where it is no longer possible to continue based on Ernst Lambert's notes, here they end. It is only known that he spent the second half of the summer in his country home, its garden overgrown with wormwood and shabby gazebo, while patching and upgrading – not entirely without enthusiasm –

his doctoral thesis about Estonian lichens.

He had always tried to manage his discoveries to the end – one must not be arrogant, having received kindness! – and it was no different this time. Ernst took the enamelled pail for salting mushrooms, put three shovelfuls of ashes from the hearth into its bottom and the heavy wooden lid of the jam cauldron over it. The star lay sleeping on the tin by the fireless hearth. Now it was dull and gloomy; cold and heavy. Tongs were no longer needed. Was it pretending or was its sleep really so deep, bottomless? The charges within it had found a solution, the arc-shaped beams had relaxed, the phosphorescent glitter seemed never to have happened. Ernst locked the door of the flat, and took the four-thirty sleeper-train to Tõravere.

There on the slope, breathing the clear and pure air, light like freedom, he stood on the edge of a sloping barley field, which grew into a sparse group of stacks of early harvested rye. That rye was still tied together in stacks! Signs of the departing summer, as well as the departing era.

The summer was blazing its last hours before dying. It was difficult to think of its black evenings as belonging together with the glistening white and still-tranquil days of high summer. Still long and striped with swallows. And so there was enough light to notice anything, particularly if on top of the hill, beyond which the domes of the observatory were shining like three bald heads, frenetic building work was going on with carpenters' hammers banging.

But the three bald heads against the background of a bone-coloured sky did not look asleep at all. And who could have feigned tranquillity while surrounded by such noise of machines, commotion and bustle of hoists, which felt deafening in the end-of-summer tranquillity. The work was only just reaching full swing, just now a stone base was being built for the guest house of the conference centre.

Having waited until the mason with his headphones and orange protective helmet stepped aside for a moment to catch a word from his mobile phone through the boom of the cement mixer, Ernst slid the piece of star out of the bucket and lifted it onto the pile of nice granite stones next to the working face. A stone among stones! Still looking at the phone screen the mason closed the phone, grabbed the top stone from the pile, threw in some mortar, and the piece of bolide was in the wall. With a whistle, the young builder added another, the third stone, many stones – earthly ones – to the stone from the sky.

The stone wall was growing quickly. There it was, somewhere. Who knows, today still in the safe carry-cot of sleep, if anything is ever going to quiver awake in it? When the sky fills with stars again on August nights, perhaps a knowing eye will catch a small longing glow down here, on Tõravere hill?

Now Ernst knew that something you must reach for in the heights can never lie on the ground by your feet as a simple find. What has to be earned as a whole, cannot be a mere shard... he was walking along the hard footpath between the fields, down the hill. There was no need to hurry, the train had just gone. It wasn't the last one. And before the next train came, he would have time to think.

To think about what to say to Alexandra Dunayeva the following day, when he was going to ask if he could offer shelter for longer to the little blue-capped one, to offer him a home.

                              Käsmu, July-August 2010

Translated by Eva Finch and Jason Finch

Awakenings
Maimu Berg

During this horrid spring the thrush went silent in the park. At the same time last year it had sung from early morning till dark. I kept the window open to hear this fanfare, although chill and humidity as well as unpleasant smells occasionally came in. The triumphant call of the bird cut sharply through the city noise, making it sound secondary, ridiculous. It was a bold, proud, joyous song caring about nothing. And while I knew what wonders a nightingale could do with its throat, and, walking in the suburbs, breathing in the scent of the bird cherry, I had heard that bird at its exercises, I still admired the thrush with all my heart. And I wouldn't have dared to go to the suburbs at night to listen to the true nightingale. In my bed, falling sleep, I enjoyed the energetic, daring and naughty cry of the thrush that came in through the open window. But this spring there was no thrush. Jogging in the park in the morning I did hear birdsong: tits were chirping, wagtails squeaking, starlings were sounding off, seagulls were screaming and the finch screeched, sparrows chirruped in the shrubs, but, yes, the thrushes remained silent.

The days, although all the same, started like a poem. Sleep always ended at quarter past six. And at quarter to seven I was already in the park. There were, in fact, three parks. In the nearest one I was never alone. The caretaker was always there before me, little knitted hat on, knapsack on her back, a rake and a broom in hand. She would be picking up bigger pieces of litter with her hooked stick, sweeping the paths, raking the sprouting grass. We never exchanged looks. Had I seen the woman in another place, differently dressed, I would not have recognised her. We arranged our movements in such a way that we wouldn't have to meet each other on a path. Who knows if, say, it's suitable to greet a person whom you meet every morning, more often than your friends and relatives? My father had lived in Kadriorg before the war and when he went to school in the morning, sometimes the President was sitting on the park bench, hat on and walking stick beside him. And my father greeted him politely, raising his school cap, to which the president raised his hand to his hat and greeted him back. It was easier with the President: everyone knew him. Accepting a greeting was part of his job. It was different with a caretaker; her work was something else and she didn't necessarily like to be disturbed. So as not to make things too awkward, I soon moved on to the next park, which was usually empty of people. Only the occasional jogger ran through. Even these were always the same ones: a woman in a white cap, a man in a blue raincoat and a tall, old athlete well known to my generation, in faded leggings and t-shirt. There was also the fourth one – a man was standing at the top of the tower, waiting until the church bell started ringing seven. At the very first strike he made the flag ascend and the trumpets play the first bars of the anthem.

    I ran up to the moat, where a young father appeared every morning, pushing a pram. He turned up precisely when the last sound of the anthem had just dispersed in the air, leaving

Baltic Belles

behind a tinny hum, but the air was still quivering. He never looked round, his gaze remained on the pram, but I suspected there was no baby in it. The father, or whatever he was, sped round with the pram along the park paths, coat flying around him. He climbed up the steep slope of the moat, balanced on the narrow path high above the water and charged down on the other side, where there was no path at all. The pram bounced over the tree roots and rocks: any child would have started crying at that, but no sound came. And if there was someone in the pram, the social services should have been informed about a father like this and his crazy storming around. But all such communications had been made too complicated recently. They ended up with you finding out that you yourself were the guilty one. Therefore I put my headphones on and started to listen to one of my favourites, Bela Bartók's *Concerto for Orchestra*. It was at times quite good music for jogging and sometimes allowed you to walk, too.

Squirrels were chasing each other up and down the oak tree, little birds were looking for food in the grass. You had to watch your step carefully, as after another heavier rainstorm there were plenty of pools and puddles, but then again the shrubs were green now and the buds were about to flower. Everything was so secure, eternal and safe, as if a big war was about to start. The same plants were sprouting in the park that I remembered from my early childhood: pilewort, coltsfoot, white nettle, dandelion. This permanence of familiar plants, every spring, every summer is like a sign of the perishability of life, of the fact that among those eternally unchanging blades of grass, blossoms and leaves coming and going I was temporary, accidental. This time I was here, but there were

Baltic Belles

thousands of others before me, as well as after me. The church bells striking every quarter of an hour only reinforced that feeling. Bartók's music got too restless. Sometimes music comes too close...

Only last week I'd watched drakes fighting over a female duck. The water churned around the angry birds and they were also hissing at the agitated female a little way away, until she took off with a flutter, the male ones at her tail. But by now the ducks had coupled. One couple was particularly bold. They were napping on the high bank of the moat, heads under wings. But getting closer I saw that the male one's head was sticking out just enough to show his dark eyes, looking at me vigilantly. I slowed down; the ducks didn't go away. The other time they were sitting at the same place, both alert, looking down at the station and chatting quietly with each other.

Vello was also always there. I called him that because I didn't know his real name. I hadn't even seen his face properly. Vello slept on a park bench sheltered by the bushes where the early morning sun shone gentle warmth onto him. Sleeping like a baby. He must have headed out of the homeless shelter early in the morning. He was wearing a discoloured leather jacket, trousers encrusted with filth, and worn trainers. His hand, wearing a mitten, was squeezed between his legs and the other one was under his head. An unshaven chin showed above his raised collar and grey matted curls stuck out of an old woolly hat. He looked like a little boy who had nodded off while playing, without washing his feet, ears and teeth. Once he had also been a little boy, fallen asleep on the floor, whose mother gently covered him with a blanket, unwilling to wake the little fellow, too big to be picked up and carried to bed.

But one morning all was different. The caretaker wasn't there. The little park was empty and messy, plastic cups, bottles and bags were dolefully rolling around in the morning breeze. The paths had not been raked; the edges of the sandpit had not been swept. Toys abandoned by children were lying around in the sandpit. In the next park an unfamiliar grey-haired woman in a black tracksuit jogged towards me instead of the usual runners. She had the stiff movements of an elderly person. When I got to the park by the moat, I saw the familiar pair of ducks pottering in the puddle on the path. The female one was holding up her leg. She cautiously put it on the ground but seemed almost unable to step on it. She only took a couple of very effortful duck steps. Some new characters had appeared in the moat: three black and white goldeneyes were swimming around in a rakish and haughty manner, in their midst a red-headed female conscious of her importance. The ducks were standing on the bank and watching them, envious and confused, the way locals look at foreigners who can afford to take it easy and who exude the inviting mystery of much better places. I saw the familiar pram approaching, only this time it wasn't pushed by the father, but instead by a young blonde woman. So she would be the mother. She was walking in a calm and measured way along the park path, but a baby's demanding cries could be heard from the pram.

All this wasn't at all to my liking. I jogged up to the bench where Vello used to sleep, but there was no one among the bushes. The bench itself was no longer even where it had been. It had been moved to the edge of the path, in a place open to the wind and where everyone could see it. Vello was still there, however. He was crouching on the bench; naturally, he couldn't sleep in such a place. I took a seat next to Vello. He straightened up, shifted to the very end of the bench and regarded me sideways, thinking that I didn't notice. "Your bed is gone," I said, trying to be friendly but not sympathetic. "That was to be expected," Vello replied with a voice croaky from the cold, then started to cough and spit, turning his back to me. This might have been out of courtesy, but it might also have been a sign for me to leave, but I stayed there, ignoring the smell, the repulsive stench of urine coming from Vello. What must his internal organs have looked like, a rotten brain, a swollen liver making its last efforts, a worn-out pancreas, kidneys barely able to filter salts and acids, lungs dirty and ripped, and the unhappy heart working hard between them, not knowing whether it is worth making an effort for all this. "But we can lift the bench back there, I'll help."

In actual fact, I would've liked to tease the mean and bad-tempered caretaker of the moat park. I'd kept my eye on her. It must have been her who dragged Vello's bench to this windy and busy place, and perhaps it was her too, who kicked the female duck. "No point," Vello said, flapping his palm and pulling his hat more firmly onto his head. "It will only cause trouble."

"But it was such a nice place for you to sleep."

"Nice or not, one has to rest somewhere."

"Haven't you got a home to rest in?"

To that Vello said nothing. I thought he'd nodded off again, but when I looked at him, I realised that he had kept his eye on me the whole time and now swiftly turned his gaze away. This glance, even though I only saw it for a moment, gave me a fright. Had I known this person once? Eyes are what change the least. There was something familiar in Vello's eyes. Wasn't that...? But then Vello would have recognised me, too. Is that why he was trying to cover his face with his shabby hat? No, this was definitely him and his name wasn't Vello. This was Allan. He clearly spotted that I had recognised him, slowly got onto his feet, picked up his plastic bag from under the bench and got ready to go.

"Allan," I whispered. Allan started up and tried to escape as quickly as his badly swollen legs could carry him. I followed him, grabbed his leather jacket and turned him around to face me. A foul, powerful stench hit me, but I didn't care. We faced each other for a moment, then Allan tried to release himself, but I was stronger, although the disgusting smell was nauseating. Blackened stumps of teeth were visible inside Allan's half-open mouth, his unwashed face was unsightly, swollen; never had I seen such a person as close to as this.

"Let me go, let me go, I'm not who you think I am!"

"Not any more, I suppose," I said with disgust and let go of him. But he didn't leave. He looked at me and the eyes in his stubbled face filled up with tears, the face screwed up in an unpleasant crying grimace.

"No one has spoken to me politely in years," he wailed through his drunken tears, "but then a person comes along who can speak to me like an old mate, who speaks to me respectfully."

"You have no home, then?" I asked and took his hand. He cried even harder, his nose dripped, snot falling in drops into his beard, onto his lips, and he licked it away. I recalled that somebody somewhere had talked at length about Allan's decline, how he'd lost everything, because he was gentle, trusting and weak-willed. Yes, that's what he was like. I remembered it myself, just as I remembered his home where he carried on living, alone, after his parents' death. I had visited it a few times when everything was still well or more or less alright. Allan's father, who in his time had been quite a high-up KGB hustler, had obtained this flat; the block in a quiet quarter of the city centre was full of similar types. The flats were large, with spacious rooms; even the kitchen and the bathroom, the pokiest rooms in the kind of Soviet concrete block housing that I lived in. Allan's parents had been residing abroad for some time, his father was on the list as something to do with the Russian embassy (Soviet of course). I never met him, but Allan's exotic-looking mother was beautiful in her elegant way, although perhaps a bit too extravagant for Soviet times. And then they had died one after the other and things also started to change. Allan, a good but shiftless musician, didn't have a steady job and was therefore unable to buy the luxury flat from the state when it was privatised. He tried to swap it for a smaller and cheaper one, all sorts of friends and frauds sprung up, until Allan with his remaining instruments landed up in a one-room den in a decaying wooden building. Money, quite a bit of which had passed through his fingers, had abandoned Allan. Women, especially the sort that Allan might have liked, got fewer and fewer around him. And then they were gone altogether. From time to time Allan made an effort to somehow keep his head above water. He tried to stop drinking and got together with a woman called Helle, older than him and unspoilt by beauty, who got this softie under control for a while. The flat got cleaned up, Allan's clothes were looked after, nice meals and flowers appeared on the table, and Helle found some parties where Allan was able to earn money with his music. That was a mistake, no point going on about it, everybody knows how those things work. At those parties they got Allan drunk, at home Helle got angrier and uglier by the day. Helle is still there, cleaning the same little park where I ran in the morning and for some time, she even carried a few sandwiches for Allan in her rucksack, but they no longer lived together, she didn't let Allan into the flat and soon she stopped bringing sandwiches, too. Helle had a new life, she kept away from Allan and his former home, and the little park became taboo for Allan.

"I've been dreaming of mother all the time, lately," Allan moaned. "She's probably expecting me to join her."

"There's no hurry with that," I tried to comfort him. "Have you drawn a line under everything, don't you hope for anything, expect anything, dream of anything any more?" Allan looked at me, his tears had dried, and snot was glistening in his beard.

"You're talking in such a sophisticated way... there is one thing, of course, music." He started bawling again.

"God yes, music, you used to be quite a distinguished musician. Even playing in the street could've made you a bit of money." Allan sighed.

"If only I got to a concert once more. Music can be heard here and there but I'd like to see it, too, I'd like to see the conductor, the symphony orchestra, all of the sections, the violins and violas, the cellos and the double bass..." His voice broke into crying, turning into an incomprehensible grunt. Talking about things that had remained distant from him, talking about anything exhausted him. He staggered back to the bench and crashed down onto it. His head nodded onto his chest, for a moment I thought he'd died, but soon snoring could be heard. I left Allan on the bench to sleep and ran towards home, Allan's smell of dirt and urine in my nostrils. Then the thrush started to sing.

The concert hall was almost full. I had bought the tickets so that Allan was sitting in the corner, right by the door, and I was next to him. All this had been a lot of hassle, and I regretted having taken on the whole thing. Cleaning and domesticating Allan, getting clothes for him from a charity shop, with major setbacks from time to time. But I had promised myself that I would take Allan to the concert and there we were now. On the stage before us were all of the instruments that Allan had dreamed about, mumbling. If he really had. Sometimes it seemed to me that he could no longer understand a thing, that he didn't know who he was or who I was, or why all this was being done to him. People pity circus elephants, but if taming an elephant is anything like as difficult as moulding Allan into a human being, it's the animal handler who should be pitied. The thing responsible for all this was my boredom, pushing me to find new challenges. Not my good compassionate heart. My heart felt for the limping duck more than for Allan, who only had himself to blame for his downfall.

The beginning of summer was warm and gentle, and Allan was itching to get back to the park, where it would be nice to take a nap in the sun, in a pleasantly enervating drunkenness. Yes, you may feed a wolf if you like, but it will still feel the pull of the forest. I was no longer bored. I would have liked to travel to the country or take a room for a week in some spa, arrange saunas, masseuses, swimming pools, jacuzzis, aromatherapy to pamper myself. But I have always adhered to the slogan from my Soviet school days – one must not leave a task unfinished. Allan was my task, my project, the culmination of which would be taking a gentleman to hear a symphony. I had rented a studio flat with a shower cabin for Allan and called in there as much as I could to keep an eye on my 'project'. But I had no intention of carrying on spending money on this in the autumn. Keeping Allan like a dog would've been the easiest and the cheapest solution. Provided he was able to behave like a dog. If he'd been quiet, sober, kept clean, come out for a walk happily and accepted walking on a leash. On the other hand, things had been getting better little by little. Allan had started to have showers, do the washing-up and change his underwear. As a prize, I got him a radio. Time passed, was spent on tedious conversations, cleaning and tidying and constant reminders of life's rules and regulations. The objective was to make Allan fit for a concert. I felt like Professor Higgins. But it was harder for me, the more so because our largely middle-aged and elderly concert audience certainly included those who remembered Allan as a musician and even recognised him. Especially now that Allan had finally agreed to have a haircut and a shave.

When Allan and I entered the large foyer of the concert hall, he was moved. We stopped at the big mirror to comb our hair and tidy up, and for the first time I looked at Allan not as a project in hand but as a human being, perhaps even as a man. Allan's eyes still had bags under them. Well, I too had bags under my eyes, although I hadn't drunk aftershave or slept on park benches. Allan's cheeks had hollowed; his face was no longer swollen. A martyr's expression had appeared in his eyes. It was apparent from his physiognomy that this character had been staring at the bottom of a glass for a good part of his life, but maybe only to me, because I knew the story. Moreover, one had to bear in mind that Allan was of quite an advanced age, an age by which one is in any case more or less battered. However, despite his age Allan had really nice curly hair, and it wasn't even completely grey, only streaked with grey, which, if we believe Jaan Kross, signals non-Estonian genes. Also, now that he was able to straighten up, it became clear that Allan was a tall, slim man, on whom even the cheap dark suit from Humana came across as elegant. At any rate, we were noticed, especially as I had several acquaintances there, and soon I observed that a few contemporaries seemed to have recognised a former musician in Allan.

In the first part of the concert they played Shostakovich's *Seventh* and in the second part the *Eighth Symphony*. In the interval there was a debate in the concourse over which of the symphonies was more powerful, a bigger success. Straight after the first bars I kept watching Allan. He was listening intently, even happily, was staring at all the instruments lovingly, the way he had dreamed on the park bench, crying. Anyway, I was bothered by his presence, knowing that I had arranged all this and that I had done it out of boredom, tedium, shortage of things to do, cold egotism, and now I was pondering intensely about what to do with Allan next. I knew nothing about his financial situation. Perhaps some little pension was coming into his bank account. I hadn't searched his filthy rags before putting them into the bin: in one of the pockets there might have been a bank card. When I mentioned this to Allan, he said that he knew nothing and had zero income. There was also the question of the dentist: I didn't want to pay to sort out Allan's mouth and the cheaper option wouldn't have been much of a solution. I suggested that Allan shouldn't laugh with his mouth wide open in decent company, should that be something he happen to find himself in.

"Don't worry," Allan replied. "Nothing makes me laugh any more."

"But you've still got your emotions, you shed tears at anything." That was indeed so: as soon as I said it, Allan started crying again.

For the concert I had stuck a cloth hanky into his breast pocket, like a gentleman should wear it, but in his pocket I put paper tissues, loose, without packaging, so he wouldn't make a crackling noise during the concert. Now the first tissue was put into use: the lyrical intro of Shostakovich's *Seventh* made Allan cry, but to his credit it has to be said that he tried to cry noiselessly and even wipe his nose quietly. This wasn't the same down-and-out who had been dribbling snot into his beard in the park. Or rather it was, of course. Although the *Seventh* was one of my favourites, it didn't do anything for me this time. I watched Allan swaying along with the well-known 'Invasion' theme. It unnerved me to think what would happen during the interval.

As soon as the applause ended, Allan and I slipped out of the door, but alas, right in front of us there was the buffet with rather a plentiful alcohol selection. Still, Allan didn't seem to notice, he'd got over his tears and now hurried to the window to settle there. He was anxious, turned his back to the concert goers walking around in the foyer and gazed intently at the street. This, of course, didn't save us. Now one of my jovial acquaintances, everybody's friend as there are in social groups, was patting me on my shoulder.

"Listen, tell me," he went on, "Tell me, is this really Allan! Sorry, Allan, if this is really you, I apologise but I thought you were long dead." And he burst out laughing, nervously.

Allan turned his martyr's face to the intruder and said in a gloomy tone, "Of course I'm dead," and turned his back again.

The jovial friend was seriously startled and asked me in a whisper, "Is this really Allan?" I nodded. "So, he's all right now?" the man carried on whispering. I shrugged, "As you see."

Other acquaintances weren't as frank. That nice Varusk couple were approaching us. Mrs Varusk with her slight limp reminded me of the lovely female duck who had nested by the moat in spring, in a good way, of course. She stopped at us, tugged at her husband and looked at us with bright eyes.

"It's you, Allan, how nice to see you after such a long while. You're an expert: which is your favourite, the *Seventh* or the *Eighth*?" It was fascinating to observe Allan opening up. How he immediately liked Mrs Varusk, or had liked her already in his former life. And how he, expertly indeed, started to analyse the *Seventh*, the so-called *Leningrad Symphony*, and the *Eighth*; how he said that he preferred the latter, especially its second and third movements, which he said that he was now looking forward to. I had nothing left to do but converse about 'weather and literature' with Mr Varusk. But the conversation was not going well, I felt with horror that I hadn't made a Galatea or turned Eliza into a lady, but instead I had brought to life a Frankenstein's Monster, which could act completely unpredictably and which couldn't be pushed back into any bottle. Or if anywhere, then precisely into a bottle perhaps.

It was unnerving to observe Allan's response to the *Eighth Symphony*. Tears were no longer flowing. Making powerful sounds he pressed his lips together, tensed his cheek muscles and looked round threateningly. I feared that he would jump up any moment and charge at someone. The drums were thundering. At the back of the orchestra a long-haired lad struck the cymbals together and a pretty young lady shook something resembling a tambourine. The squeal of the strings cut straight into your heart. The music was elevating, tragic, terrifying. Maybe Allan should have poured out his catharsis in an extreme way. After everything he had gone through. But then there was a pause, the musicians shuffled their sheets around and then the music became peaceful, to me almost boring. Allan's face relaxed and a contented smile, or what is usually referred to as a blissful smile, appeared on his lips. When the music finally gave way to silence and the hall went quiet before the applause, Allan suddenly grabbed my hand and squeezed it hard. Then he joined in with the thunderous ovation. The audience were cheering and stamping their feet, a barbaric practice in my opinion, and Allan clapped his hands together so hard that I covered my ears. On our way to the cloakroom, still on the stairs, several of our acquaintances and semi-acquaintances pushed towards us, smiled at Allan, waved to us. Society seemed to be happy with Allan. I guess none of them had seen him the way I had: sleeping on the park bench, bearded, soaked in urine, stinking. Or if they had, they hadn't recognised him. Goddamn it, I had dragged him up from the bottom, now those smiling and waving complacent characters should do something as well: they should help the man on in life, find him a flat and a job, or sort out his pension. They should have teeth put in the fellow's mouth. Straightaway tomorrow I will make it clear to Allan that now that I've helped him fulfil his dream, my protecting hand is no longer there above his curly head. I had wasted a good portion of my life on him, never mind a good sum of money. Bright-eyed Mrs Varusk, this limping duck, was making her way towards us, her dim-witted husband and a few more people behind her. What if I left Allan in their hands and went home? For some time, I hadn't gone running in the morning, I knew nothing about what was going on out there in nature; the birds were going to leave for the south soon, but I hadn't even got to the city outskirts yet to listen to the nightingale, nor had I been to the Botanical Gardens, where another queen of the night was about to bloom. I was no longer myself. I had become a carer, an animal handler, a coach, a cleaner. I'd had enough. When the people formed a circle around me and Allan, just like hunters pursuing particularly dangerous and intelligent game, I smiled, or in fact bared my teeth, and with this cruel grimace, hopefully taken for a smile by the others, announced that I was in a hurry and that I was leaving Allan, this prodigal son, in the hands of friends.

"No, don't go, wait, I'll come with you," Allan whispered and grabbed my hand. But I freed myself abruptly and elbowed my way out of the circle.

It was getting dark outside. The asphalt smelled of dust and humidity. The streetlights came on with a sudden flash, the treetops cast pattern-like shadows on the pavement. I didn't have far to go. I couldn't walk fast; I was afraid to twist my ankle in some crack in the pavement. My untrained body was clumsy and awkward. Sitting in the concert I'd noticed that my belly had gathered fat because it had been comfortable to support the crossed hands on it – this I hadn't experienced before. My feet, squeezed by my fancy patent leather shoes, were hurting. Also, the heart ached a bit. Because of Allan.

Next morning I forced myself up early and went running. The summer was over, the leaves were falling, twirling mysteriously, as if hinting at something; the ducklings that were so cute in early summer had grown into ugly stupid young ducks, who were quacking angrily and were fighting for pieces of white bread, which an old woman was throwing to them. The running was tough, my heart was pounding, my head was sweating under the woolly hat and every now and then I found myself walking. I'd used to enjoy my morning runs, I looked round me, my legs were light and it felt good. Now I was stumbling and staring around my feet trying to avoid slipping on acorns, tree roots, conkers or gravel. Migratory birds were setting off on their journey. The wagtails who had been scampering around my feet in spring, the male one, shaking his wings, approaching the female, were nowhere to be seen; now they and their young were on their way to Africa.

Thrushes were pecking around in the grass, but they remained quiet. Dark and dull, they scurried fast, suddenly turning up in unexpected places and then dispersing like frightened mice. The shadows of trees had turned sombre and long, and a white-grey mist was hovering above the pond. Someone had painted a sneering face on the stump of a sawn-off bough. There were no runners or walkers in the vicinity, no one was crouching on the benches, but some human activity had taken place here: empty vodka bottles, beer cans and ketchup-stained food boxes were lying here and there.

The dull autumn days rolled on. I hadn't heard much of Allan after our concert visit. And how would I have done? I didn't socialise much, I've never had friends. One semi-acquaintance who I randomly met in the market found it necessary to tell me Allan's story as a particular phenomenon; he didn't seem to know about my part in the story. I supposed that Allan was alive and kicking if it was true that he'd become a phenomenon. Or a curiosity.

The autumn got more and more intrusive. Somewhere nearby the first snow was said to have come down. I surfed online, searching for cheap flights to Las Palmas to winter there, to rent a room or a small flat and somehow make it till spring. The thought of the imminent winter, cold, dark and slippery, brought about more repulsion in me than the overcrowded beaches of the Canary Islands.

At home I started the day by winding up the walk clock and adjusting its hands so that the time was right. In the evening I always stopped the clock, so its striking would not wake me at night, although the clock wasn't in the bedroom. Starting this way every morning and ending every evening, it finally filled me with horror to think how short and empty the day had been in between. I started to observe how many pointless landmarks the day included. The so-called morning procedures, which used to be included in a school pupil's recommended schedule – waking, morning exercises, washing, breakfast. Taking the same route to work, whether by car or walking, but always feeling myself to be in a deep rut. And the same faces, the same conversations, the same morning newspapers with the same news in them. However, this was still a bit better than the kind of routine where work and life no longer belonged. The life of a rentier, especially with a relatively poor income, wasn't that great, but I couldn't find any use for myself, either. I didn't want to work for somebody else, and I didn't know how to run my own business. A long time ago, at a party where Allan was also present, someone had asked: what would you like to be? Everybody had then said something, I no longer remember what, but Allan said that he'd like to be a rentier, and when my turn to answer came, I said that I might be a rentier's spouse. Couldn't think of anything better. Allan had, in fact, become a rentier of sorts, a free man independent of the times. Actually entirely free because he was not chased by the ringing of a mobile phone, and the Internet didn't harass or tempt him. Allan had been a man without a phone number, without a Facebook account or an e-mail address. He read newspapers when he found them in a bin, before laying them onto the park bench to go to sleep on them.

In Las Palmas I also tried out the life of a tramp, although I had rented some accommodation quite cheaply on the outskirts. I simply missed the last bus from the beach to the city. I debated whether to lie down among the famous dunes, a naturist and gay paradise in the daytime, or to choose some decent-looking bench and spend the night dozing on that. With safety in mind, I chose the bench, but it was hard, and as I had nothing to spread out on it, the cold wind attacked me – the nights weren't particularly warm there. It turned out to be a long, dark and torturous night, during which I also had to hide from the police a couple of times. In the morning I looked at my swollen face in the mirror of the bus-station toilet; one night had been enough to make me look like a complete down-and-out. This was, in fact, the only night that stuck in my memory from my long period of vegetation in Las Palmas. No one contacted me from my home country, at the beginning I shuffled actively around on the Delfi and Postimees websites and even spotted Allan in some society chronicle. There was a reception, party or picnic somewhere, and in one photo of the Varusk couple I found Allan. He was staring at Mrs Varusk with humble and admiring doggy eyes. Allan and the Varusks were in the photo thanks to a blonde stupid-faced girlie, who was the only celebrity out of the four and who was referred to as 'our beloved weather girl' in the caption. I didn't have a clue what weather girl meant, whether she was somehow in the hands of the elements or somehow worldly or something even dodgier. Once I had read a children's story where the protagonist had been a weather girl, or more precisely, I think, Miss Weather Nose; this was otherwise a beautiful paper doll, but she had a big ugly nose that forecasted the weather. It worked so that the doll was hung on the window and its nose changed colour according to the air pressure and humidity, turning sometimes purple like blueberry soup, then again pink or light blue. I had never seen such a wonder in real life.

Spring arrived this year as well and there was no point wasting it in a place where the seasons were barely detectable. On the third day back in my homeland, in a shopping centre café, I met an acquaintance, an old party hack who knew everybody and everything. I asked him all mealy-mouthed about Allan, too.

"Good old Allan!" he cried, as if giving a headline for the account that was to follow. Those headlines he had, were in fact all the same: good old, followed by a name. "Well, after the scandal no one has heard of him."

"What scandal?"

"You don't know? Where have you been?" This was the first question anybody asked about my life, but it wasn't meant to be answered. "The Varusks' scandal." I didn't want to interrupt him with questions and he told a story about how Mrs Varusk had been having it off with Allan, how for some time the three of them, the Varusks and Allan, lived together. "Good old Varusk, henpecked and foolish, a disgrace to manhood, and then that woman…"

"The limping duck," I said, I thought so quietly that my interlocutor wouldn't have heard it, but he exclaimed, "The limping duck, you say! Yes, but there is something in that woman, something… if there is a limping duck in that family, it's old Varusk himself. In any case, a love triangle formed there." And he started to describe that triangle to me in detail. I was half-listening. Some people were still able to fall in love, form triangles, experience heartache, to suffer. From love, from jealousy! Empty days between two windings of the clock and a great love that fills your day and night, night and day, until there is no difference between them, no mornings or evenings, and this was experienced by Allan, my Frankenstein's Monster, the bum from the park bench. "But then old Varusk had enough. He grabbed a stool to knock his head open, and the woman was screaming beside them."

"He killed Allan?"

"No, the other way round."

"Allan killed Varusk?"

"Oh, there's Grisha, good old Grisha, hey, come here!" And he waved to a tall man in a light-coloured raincoat, whose face was flushed as if he had just come from the sauna.

"Did Allan kill Varusk?"

"Of course not," my interlocutor said casually and then focused on 'good old' Grisha.

Next morning I went running in the park for the first time in a good while. I felt in quite good shape. The sun was shining and Helle the caretaker was pottering round in the small park, her rucksack on her back and perhaps even sandwiches for someone in it. Birds were singing and the thrush was sounding louder than the other birds. A woman in a white cap ran towards me and gave me an interrogating look. I got a glimpse of the old athlete in the bushes like a large greying elk. Drakes were looking for food in the pond and gave sidelong jealous looks at the couple nodding off in the sunshine on the bank – that particular male had managed to win over a female. The same plants were sprouting and springing up, the same squirrels were chasing each other up and down the tree and the same conkers I had stumbled on in the autumn, now black after the winter, were lying on the path. Nothing had changed. Or there was something. At the other end of the pond a stripy plastic police tape had been drawn across the path and something could be seen lying on the grass. Apparently a person. A dead person. A corpse. I wanted to go under the tape but the policeman stopped me.

"What happened here?"

The policeman didn't answer, but a man in a blue jacket, whom I remembered from my runs the previous spring, explained, "He was pulled out of the water. He'd either fallen in or been pushed in."

"Who was it?"

"Don't know, looks like a homeless guy." I craned my neck to look, but nothing much could be seen. The face of the body had been covered with a filthy wet jacket. I don't know if it seemed to me or if I really saw greying hair sticking out under the jacket. Salt and pepper, like that of people who have alien, non-Estonian genes.

A week later I saw the Varusks in the street. The man had his arm around the woman's shoulders and she looked up at him, licking her ice cream. They were walking slowly and it seemed to me that the man was limping. It was the first heat wave of the spring.

2015

Translated by Eva Finch and Jason Finch

At the Manor, or Jump into the Fire
Maarja Kangro

She hoped the pianist would grab the other *cabanossi* sausage for himself. Who could tell what Bulgarian horsemeat it was made of – what reason would she have for trusting Statoil more than anyone else? It actually tasted like horsemeat to her, and although this *cabanossi* might not have been horse, and definitely wasn't quality horse, she was now bolting it down as if she were starving. But the other *cabanossi* was for the pianist after all. The pianist had to take it himself, into his supple, intelligent fingers. It was April and the litter had melted away, the brightly-coloured flying silver of tramps and local schoolchildren. The pianist smiled and said that his stomach wasn't empty yet. Did the manor house have no badger parfait to offer them?

At the manor, at the manors. Some manors. Look how versatile the word manor is. The ladies of the manor, manor work-days, cabbage-soup-scented manor schools where the children blew their noses on the curtains.

"What are you on about?" said the girl flautist. "They're so beautifully restored, some of them really tastefully."

"Listen, in Soviet times they really did blow their noses on them," said the poet. "On the curtains. In the early years of my life I was actually a boarder at a manor school."

She'd actually blown her nose on a rag, or a red Pioneer

Baltic Belles

kerchief, but if the rag stuffed in the drawer was already so full of snot that she could wipe no more with it, she, the class monitor, did wipe her snotty hands on the curtains. From the window bedecked by the curtain on which the poet had wiped her snotty, chalky hands, from that window some lovestruck Mathilde must once have stared into the river valley in her inept musings.

Manor tourism. The mobile homes with yellow Dutch number plates in the yard, because no Dutchman is fool enough to shell out for a *deluxe* suite. *Small luxury hotel.* Wow, the lawn is velvet-smooth, the lovely robot mows it, but the kitchen dupes you with fresh plaice, so it thrives.

"One of these plasterboard rooms at a manor house out in the sticks recently cost us more than a hotel in central Rome," said the poet.

"Really," said the pianist.

"Sixty-four," said the poet. "Sixty-four euros for a single and ninety for a twin room, in a manor house in the middle of nowhere."

Oh yes, the Baltic Germans left us some architectural gems, no doubt about it. The lady of the manor, dressed in a green outfit with puffed sleeves, brings your tea to the table, it's herbal tea, she picked some fresh peppermint here just now, hot water on top and there you go, but it's not included in the price, only four euros. Boiled eggs – you don't always get them for breakfast in Mediterranean countries, honestly.

The poet took a sip from the bottle of mineral water she was offered.

But write up a study of the Baltic Germans and it will be a sensation, nominate it for a prize and you might even win.

Baltic Belles

What they all wrote here and daubed on canvas, what they wore and ate and how they behaved on the toilet, just think, they shat here in these very chamber pots. No, of course, I'm saying nothing about where we might have got this stuff, what else would we put on the sweet tins if the gentlemen hadn't painted pictures. The Baltic Germans' yarns, all their yarns, all the delicate threads that bind the Baltic German identity – they could be translated into Estonian and at least be published in *Looming* magazine's Library Series, couldn't they. Ah, what do we have! We have Bellingshausen, we have Hermann von Keyserling, we have, we have Uexküll, by God, Uexküll!

The musicians laughed.

"By the way, though," said the violinist, "last year there was a case like that. A whole article came out, about how a Baltic German lady was coming to the K Festival. The lady's husband was playing the flute at the festival. But the article was about the lady and her family tree, of course, not about the flautist."

"In other words, a Baltic German crosses the news threshold," said the pianist.

"What the fuck," said the poet. The musicians laughed again; she finished the second *cabanossi* and wrapped the remaining hunk of bread in paper.

And when we have foreign visitors, then wherever are we going to take them? Farmhouse or manor house, if you please. At a little farmhouse, jellied herring with poisonous Chinese cabbage brought straight from Spain, nine euros. Or how about the hunting lodge with roast wild boar with local wild-berry preserve, thirty-three euros plus seasonal salad, four euros fifty, perhaps with that same Chinese cabbage, that would be nice, but among the pigskins and stags' heads there is a gang of grumbling middle-aged Finns. Meanwhile let's look over the graveyard. How they were all there, sitting in their little terraces drinking tea, and now they are lying under their heavy headstones. Where in their hearts were they any worse than us? How much can we manage to do for our own social formation, eh?

But that time, when we'd had enough of looking at those hunting halls and rose gardens and duck ponds, and the foreign visitors had shrugged, because their own oppressors' luxury was on a far greater order of magnitude, and in one hall I had found, on the flanks of an exhibited uniform worn by the lord of the manor, a plastic button marked *Made in Uruguay,* I told my dear colleague H that I would be leaving now, I'd skip the Manorisms and the Baltic Germanisms, and H said he would come too, and yeah, he was starting to feel like a manor arsonist. That was a beautiful spring-like moment: feeling like a manor arsonist.

The violinist smiled. "You have a sort of Estonian genetic hatred," he said.

"Genetic," repeated the poet. "I don't know. And what's this 'Estonian' – *c'mon.* Things like that are global. The little lord-gods. What shall I do with this hunk of bread?"

"Look, back there is one of Rademar's bags," said the violinist.

"As a child," said the poet, "as a child I dreamed several times that I was a Teutonic Knight. I was tied into the ground with a stake, and I understood that this was right."

"How old were you then?" asked the pianist.

"Well, only ten or so. I suppose I'd been reading stories

about my country's history and masterpieces like *The Time of the Wolf's Law.*"[4]

"Poor child," said the pianist.

"Oh," said the poet, "you've seen that, have you? I thought not many people knew it."

"Was Meleleiv in it?" asked the pianist.

"Yeah, right," said the poet, *"yeah,* Meleleiv! Men in coarse clothes, with long hair, with synth music. That's the image of Estonians from my childhood."

The girl flautist, who was too young to remember Meleleiv, said: "They've given plenty to us, I mean the Baltic Germans. Where would we be without them – melted into the Slavic peoples?"

"Isn't our culture a Baltic German invention after all?" said the violinist. "Didn't Herder make it up?"

The poet yawned.

"I know some very nice Baltic Germans," said the flautist. "Real nobility doesn't advertise itself at all."

"That beats everything!" said the poet. "Damn! It ought to be officially banned. At least the Austrians got that right, when they banned noble titles."

"And how has that helped?" said the pianist.

"Well now," said the poet, "no one has confiscated the bastards' property. And you always know when it's some noble Schwarzenberg. The mania for titles still flourishes in all that academic bullshit."

"Lord, yes," said the violinist.

"But we," said the poet, "we at least should ban titles. It

---

[4] An Estonian pseudo-historical film made in 1984, widely criticised for its implausible plot and anachronisms.

could be made so that anyone who crosses the Estonian border automatically loses all the *von*s and *zu*s and *di*s and *de*s."

"But aren't there some titles that we can't trace?" said the pianist. "You might get some Swahili princess."

"Well, Swahili," said the poet. "But you'd have to draw up a register of all the world's noble titles. Although it probably exists already somewhere. When they're issuing visas to them or when somewhere – well, let's say when they're reporting to give a performance – whoosh, off they go!" She shook her fist energetically at no one in particular. "So much for your titles!"

It was warm in the minibus, cold outside. The pianist laughed and said: "Die, dogs!"

How strange. The poet knew the pianist from before; they'd drunk wine together in the same company a couple of times. And until now she'd acknowledged him with friendly attention. Now the poet noted that the pianist was verbally skilled. She had already heard, at the petrol station, how sensitively the man used onomatopoeic words. *Trickle, chug, tatterdemalion, dangle.*

As a still very young and easily upset equal-rights activist, the owner of a fresh Soviet passport for foreign travel, still far from being a poet, she had been on her first trip to Western Europe, and in Germany the concerts were invariably at some *Schloss*, and it was there that she realised for the first time, as an unpleasant sensation, that without violence and injustice those baroque beauties would evidently never have come into being as they were, nor their ceilings grown so high. Pomposity and ornament caused embarrassment even in art books, and they were cool – without them it would have been sombre and bleak. Likewise, in her youthful atheism she had suspected that if there were no images or reminders of God, then the architecture of cities would lack a certain excitement. Now we are here, we have large palaces, with museums in them, we analyse religious vocal works, it's as if we have woken from a bad dream, but that dream, a violent dream, in which others have died – must we be thankful for it?

At one castle reception she had bitten into a decorative banana that tasted distinctly of breadcrumbs.

'Monsters,' she thought. 'Monsters, yet in their hands are the things of this world, some have larger, some have smaller things. And then those who try to ape the monsters. Yes, petty people with a thousand euros a month are now pulling black silk stockings onto their stubbly legs and going off to manor houses, and now they can even visit the gilded high-ceilinged museums of the world, if they scrimp and save, and afterwards they imagine that they've almost got to wear that pig's face, that monster's face. We want people to think we're doing well, woo-hoo, we're doing well, we're doing well!'

"The master-and-servant dialectic doesn't work any more, unfortunately," said the poet. "Poor Hegel laid it to rest."

"We just had Hegel in a seminar, and they were talking about that very idea," said the flautist. She wanted to gain a doctorate on the flute, and was on her way to getting one, never mind not knowing about Meleleiv.

"What shit," said the poet. This dialectic was a beautiful idea. The slave, who has to do the work, gets ever more skilful and wise, while the lords, who only enjoy others' achievements, gradually sink into impotent sluggishness, lose their understanding and grasp of things. Beautiful, beautiful. Actually the subordinate one doesn't learn anything, he hasn't got time to think of anything but getting by, he's like the body in the Matrix, who just gives out his energy, he doesn't have time to wake up because he doesn't have any money.

"No," said the poet, "there's no dialectical element in it; they eat frankfurters and ketchup there."

And those up there don't lavish their own power on themselves. They don't even eat fit to burst themselves any more, they eat mild vegetarian food, boiled pike-perch, but red meat, even organic, they don't eat every day by any means. No one knows how to cultivate the customs of ancient Rome any more, only a few people in the arts, and as a rule they tend to be born earlier than the eighties. They've even given up smoking.

"Is that bad?" asked the violinist. "Eating vegetarian food?"

"No," said the poet. "No. Or yes, it's bad that the dialectic doesn't work here, they don't eat till they burst."

She looked out of the bus window. It was drizzling a little; the air was brownish-grey.

Now the pianist handed her the mineral-water bottle, straight from his own mouth, and the poet smiled.

"Isn't that so? Our *own* Laocoon dumplings – that's *something*."

It was an ordinary neo-classical manor house, with six columns, and was quite recently painted whitish-grey. A large round lawn extended in front of the house, at the moment still brownish. On both sides of the lawn paved paths led to the outbuildings and on into the park.

"This one is Aili B.'s – Erato Real Estate," said the

violinist to the flautist.

Nature in April, a pre-presentiment: this pleased the poet. Maybe April was one of the most beautiful months of the year. The cruellest month, and so on.

"The family will be a little longer. I mean, the lady. The gentleman and his son are now in Greenland."

The estate manager or economic director of Manor N. smiled. He had slightly thinning hair, but for that reason American facial features, a broad smile.

"Shall we take a little tour – would you like to?"

He started explaining the history of the local manor house, and the poet watched her companions with a wry smirk. The coachhouse had now become an art gallery – half of it had, because one actual coach still remained there.

"Ah I see," said the violinist.

"The lady's Lamborghini," said the estate manager. "Haha! How many Lamborghinis are there in Estonia altogether, how many?"

They didn't know.

"The shingle roof?" asked the violinist. "Who put that on?"

"That would be the Egert Roofing Group. All of our outbuildings here have beautiful shingle roofs, the whole complex. The sports centre, the summerhouse, the garage-gallery. But we've also had problems with it, you know our people."

Right behind the gallery-garage the path went to Mr. K.'s house, and this person was causing them constant trouble here. Mr. K. was a drunk. His land couldn't be bought from him. He'd just keep going around the gallery there, smashed out of his head, and of course kick up a fuss. Last spring he claimed that some ice had fallen off the shingle roof onto his head, clumps of it had fallen onto his land. He'd come with his injured head to the manor, drunk as a lord, dripping blood.

The flautist shook her head.

"Guess he might have fallen down somewhere while sloshed," said the estate manager. "Then he started imagining things. He came staggering in with bloody clumps of ice to look at. It all melted onto our parquet floor, the blood and the ice."

He smiled and continued: "Why don't we clean the roof... but you aren't supposed to break ice on a shingle roof; that would break the roof. Of course some might fall off it in the spring, but not enough to make your head bloody. Now the man is threatening to set fire to the manor. Well, there are such sad people around. The remnants of the Soviet time, you know."

But as they were walking through the manor house corridor, the poet saw metal name-plates on the doors of the rooms: Amalie, Emilie, Charlotte, Elisabeth, Marie-Antoinette. 'What?' wondered the poet.

The April day was cold and so the pianist was wearing black leather gloves. He didn't bother to take them off to try out the piano, but made a deadly serious face and let fly with an impromptu rendering of Chopin's Fantasia in C sharp minor. The piano was bad and he gradually started to sneer. Oh, yeah! Like bright unhappy little rows of pearls the notes poured from under the black robust gloves, and the pianist just kept on grinning and the poet noticed that he also had beautifully-shaped ears. It was a known fact that true irony presupposes artistry.

At some time the poet, too, had been educated, gone to school, where through the windows sounded a secure mixture of *études* and scales, parts being constantly repeated. Even today the sound of music practice aroused a delicious feeling of guilt in her.

The pianist got up, took off his gloves and his coat; now he was in a black shirt, so his figure could be seen beautifully, and he didn't have love handles or anything. The poet wondered what would it be like if she grabbed the man by his sides, just under the ribs, above the hips, where there is only flesh. Pressed her fingers into that flesh. Moved her hand down below the man's belly, the shirt-buttons, the cloth, the warmth of the skin. The trouser-belt. It was moving the way men pull their trouser-belts tight. Covering the body was a crazy, crazy business.

Academic musical training – doesn't it raise people up to the top of the erotic rankings among the professions – right up there with doctors? Bowing on a stage in a black suit versus the white coat – which would be the winner?

They looked at the ceiling. There were art nouveau plants painted on it.

"Well, they've got money," said the poet.

"Mmm, yeah. To do whatever their hearts desire," said the pianist.

"Minimalism would have been better here," said the violinist.

"Yeah," said the pianist. "Simply bare walls, take down what comes down. Make it a skeleton, so to speak."

"Who was it who said that the more developed a culture is, the less ornamentation it has? Or in the environment?" asked the poet. "Was it Adolf Loos?"

"Minimalism is always a sure way to go," said the violinist.

"Yeah, look, I've been thinking it *always* would," said the poet. "Or can minimalism be presented as a kind of kitsch?"

"Some plywood boxes on the wall?" ventured the violinist.

And the poet agreed that, "No, it's really hard to think of those as kitsch, really formalist minimalism. But if there has to be some telling message in this reduction, this taciturnity, then there is already something pretentious," she said, and the pianist said, "Yes, deep and minimalism do mix."

"That's it," said the poet joyfully, "Deep! But deep and kitsch are related. And those holy minimalists, well, I don't know, I feel physically sick when I have to listen to something of Tavener's, as if someone were dipping me in sugar-water by force."

"That's not quite kitsch," said the violinist, "new age and not to be taken too seriously, but certainly not kitsch."

"But it's still quite hard to tolerate – I mean Tavener," said the pianist, and the poet thought that the pianist's attitude was really accurate.

"Isn't the lack of conflict in art a dubious sign, I mean, these days? Palestrina was beautiful, but now – doesn't it frighten you a bit?"

"What?" asked the violinist.

"Well, *why* do people smooth things over in their work, why do they deny unsolvable conflicts. *Why.* And anyway, isn't it arrogance toward your fellow humans to aim for sainthood, to claim holiness, in your creative work?"

"*Minimalist kitsch* – it sounds somehow familiar. Isn't there a book with that name? Or an exhibition by someone? The

Baltic Belles

Kitsch of Silence – ha!"

But the chatter had now gone from those walls to this. The violinist smirked.

"Well hello, hello."

The poet now became aware that this slight woman, with a shrill and self-assured voice, had been following them for some time from the hall door.

"Oh, hi," said the violinist, going over to give the woman his hand.

"I've been listening here to the way you keep on chatting and chatting, and I wondered if anyone's in the mood to play," said the woman. Now she stepped up to the whole group and stretched out her hand. "Aili B. Let's agree that we'll have a good concert, eh?"

The poet looked at the diminutive woman's red chamois high-heeled shoes. They were shoes by Peter Kaiser; she had a blue pair just like them at home. The woman might have been fifty, but she obviously preferred to be thought of as thirty-five. She can't be – fifty! She can, she can.

"If the audience is worth it at all, then we will," said the poet.

The woman cast her a bubbly look of acknowledgement. "The audience is top class. And the instrument's good, isn't it?" The woman knocked on the piano.

The pianist grinned. "Let's get started," he said. "We've seen everything."

The tables were laid with white tablecloths and the chairs were completely white, as pretty as corpses. The napkins were alluringly folded into wavelets, the waiters were carrying platters to the table. The dog-faced monsters sat at the white tables and talked, some of them watching the stage.

They were sitting on the stage, looking into the hall.

"We are the elite."

"We are the elite."

"We."

"We."

"We."

This was no dialogue or dispute. It was the internal sound of each side, maybe unconscious now. One businesswoman was having such a good time evidently that she allowed her nose to peel. Her outfit, too, was beige, not flag-blue or snow-white. Humourlessly, intensively, she stared toward the platform. The others were talking among themselves, maybe informally, raising their pieces of roast duck.

But some of the more aspiring businesspeople or their daughters and wives had dressed themselves in black and red, hanging fragilely on the arms of their worthy, sometimes deceived spouses. The corset and the fishtail, these are the favourites of the Estonian woman, one fashion designer had told the poet. The corset and the fishtail. What fine, clever, enterprising Estonian women, who have wandered through three-quarters of the world. The businesslike men, having found some time away from business to immerse themselves in Tibetan Buddhism or boxing, to collect the works of artists who cite the young progressives – citing not only Deleuze but also Laclaud. The poet wondered if she might have food poisoning after all.

'Bugger it,' she was already sitting there on the platform.

They had agreed that they would sit all the time in front

of the audience and she would read her own texts between the musical pieces. And only now did she come to realise what a big mistake she had made in not coming in her own car, because now she couldn't leave at a moment's notice. There she sat in a stupid pseudo-baroque pinkish armchair, which must have had a name of its own, such as *Amaliensessel* or *Theresiensessel*. If she had got up now and left the platform, that would be taking a stand, but that stand would work only if she could then start the car and disappear forever from the dog-faces of the monsters. But the red minibus that had brought them there didn't belong to the poet. Where would she have gone – into the shadows of the forest on a cold April evening, for three hours?

One man got up from the table with its white tablecloth, and now the poet understood that this was her former classmate and, for a while, gym-mate. At the age of fourteen the boy's face had become a bit flushed, and he was showing a pronounced tendency to fat. By now the ruddiness was replaced by a Dubai or Guadeloupe tan, and there was no sign of the fat. The man was working in the SEB bank's growth fund, and writing an investment blog. The poet still stubbornly believed that she herself had got further in life than her classmate.

"Hi there," said the classmate.

"Hello."

"So what are you doing here?"

"You'll see."

"Going to sing?"

"You can hope."

The classmate had perfumed himself; so had the poet.

The poet pursed her lips; the classmate smiled.

"So how's it going?" asked the poet.

"Well, let's say, quietly at the moment," said the classmate. "Now and then I keep reading the bullshit you write in the media."

"Yeah, cool. Me too, I sometimes read the bullshit you write. And you *do* it – people like you *do* bullshit. Wrecking the world, *capitalist proklyatyy*,[5] that sort of thing."

The classmate waved her away. "Maybe there'll be time to chat afterwards," he said, and went to sit in his place. Sitting next to him was a tanned girl with finely plucked eyebrows, her hair falling from a blond bun in immeasurable curly wisps onto her shoulders. 'Revolution, dammit,' thought the poet, 'Revolution. We will win, *Venceremos!*'

'What the hell. We're fucked. How much of that independence have we had, we people in the arts. Great defenders of freedom.' The poet could still feel how her colleagues in the arts loved intellectuals. 'Class-love – that's one of the few real kinds of love,' she thought, not wanting to be told what an illusion that was.

It was clear to her that she couldn't put up with much inter-class contamination.

'Some will let you in through the door,' she thought. 'We all sit in the roofed terrace or in front of the stove and sip cocktails, and the bankers tell us what new things they've read. There's no way out. Only the poor Eastern European orchestra players, yes, they, and the drunken writers and the young people in the arts, for whom red is cool one second before a commercial gallery starts marketing red as cool.'

'*Was bleibet aber, dichten die Stifter,*' as our German

---

[5] Damned capitalist (Russian).

Baltic Belles

colleagues paraphrased Hölderlin.

She was passé, an anachronism, sitting on top of a tussock, which was an old-fashioned image, from a time when the world was just mixed up and wavy. To each his own.

The violinist and the pianist were starting.

The pianist was the fourth generation of a family of musicians. Polished genes, that was obvious. Aware of his rank. He didn't scream, wasn't tense about self-assertion. He didn't sniff the wind. It was beautiful to watch him. Now the poet was looking at his neck.

And she was thinking how now and again she made the mistake of getting up to read her poetry somewhere else than in a hall of the Writers' Union with its black ceiling, somewhere else than at festivals with a specific audience. Hadn't she seen enough uncomprehending looks by now, from innocent eyes, to which she had come to offer emptiness, or at best sympathetic nihilism, but they didn't want that emptiness; they already had their teacups on the table and now she had to perform. She didn't want to scream and be dramatic here, she no longer wanted to read her poetry aloud.

The pianist finished, the poet got to her feet and yelled: "I'll read to you about a pig! Listen carefully, because the main character in this next poem is a *pig!*"

There was laughter and chuckling.

She read, not too dramatically, but intensively. Each time she said 'pig' she looked someone straight in the eyes, including her classmate.

But what she saw was that the audience's steak plates were empty, there were only fish-bones and duck-skins floating on

Baltic Belles

the dishes and side plates, and when she finished declaiming, the waiters came and took the empty plates away from the tables.

She nodded at the applause, but she didn't bow; she sat down and looked at the violinist.

"What the hell – has the food run out? Are we being taken to the kitchen afterwards to feed on leftovers?"

"My belly's pretty empty," said the violinist.

"Shall we go?" said the poet, almost out loud, and started to get up. "To hell with the badger-parfait leftovers."

"Wait," said the violinist. The pianist made a calming movement of the hand.

The girl with the flute was starting to play. The red-haired postgraduate flautist signed petitions and shared articles of a political nature on Facebook, though she didn't comment on them much.

She had hardly stopped playing when the lady of the house came, with sparkling eyes, at a brisk pace onto the dais, during the applause, *Kaiser's shoes, Kaiser's shoes*. She made a gesture to quieten the applause.

Something con-cep-tu-al she wanted now. Something shocking: well – the chatelaine smiled – something by Cage.

The poet looked at her with weary contempt.

"Play 3'44"," said her former classmate. The classmate had been worse at everything than the poet, in languages, mathematics, art history, and now he said 3'44", which wasn't right, it should be 4'33", but it was something anyway. Ah, *ressentiment*. The poet thought it was possible that one day he would die a death of reactionary annoyance, despite his low blood pressure. Maybe she should go esoteric, before it was too late.

Something con-cep-tu-al.

"Who – me?" asked the flautist. The hostess made an incomprehensible gesture. The violinist and the pianist smirked and indicated to the flautist: please, go ahead. She shrugged, saying that she had no Cage, but she could play a sequence of Berio, which she happened to have in her head.

The lady of the house didn't leave the dais, but started illustrating the piece with a hand pantomime, standing between the flautist and the audience. The poet tried to signal to the girl with the flute to stop playing, and not to let the monster desecrate it. But then she chuckled. And she looked again at those foolishly fluttering hands and chuckled again, unable to hold back her laughter.

The DJ jerked his head and body carelessly. Daft Punk's *Get Lucky*. Swaying in time to the music, the hostess approached the table, at which the poet was standing with the musicians. She was carrying a tray of cheeses, which tipped over, but the pianist skilfully avoided the accident. "Sorry, I really am. I asked the kitchen to keep back portions for you, but they must have misunderstood. But these cheeses have come from France, Italy and Holland, ordered specially for us." A Vermeer, a Cognac Bellavitano, and elegantly aged Asiago, and of course a Roquefort as well. With a toothpick the violinist popped a deep yellow piece in his mouth. No compromise, the poet decided. She would endure until the next *cabanossi*, to hell with these Asiagos. She congratulated herself. The pianist took a piece of Roquefort and the poet regarded him warmly. A sweet, childish, pragmatic person in the arts. She imagined that she was too, and did indeed take a piece – maybe it was even Asiago.

Plak-plak-plak-plak. The DJ had put a new number on: *Please don't let me be misunderstood*, as performed by Santa Esmeralda.

"Oh!" squealed the lady of the house.

She started thumping her red shoes on the floor and hysterically clapping her hands. "Wasn't she Spanish, wasn't she, eh?"

The percussive part of the music ended, but the lady kept on stumbling back and forth in front of the pianist, clapping tipsily. Then she grabbed the pianist's hand, lifted it up, and swayed around him. The pianist smirked and let it happen, half-abstractedly. When she started to fall over, the pianist caught her.

"My God," said the chatelaine. She grabbed a glass of water from the pianist and gulped from it. Then she carried on clapping and staggering.

More menacing, joyful bass lines could be heard from Santa Esmeralda. And the DJ said that with this song he was sending greetings to Meril. The poet felt a new, sharp slap of disappointment. The number was Harry Nilsson's *Jump into the Fire* and this was her favourite song from her early teenage years – nobody else owned that old Nilsson record *Son of Dracula*, and this was her splendid experience of being different. When Scorsese had used that song about jumping into the fire in his *Goodfellas*, the poet had been slightly offended, because that put her childhood number into wider circulation, but Scorsese was after all an intelligent person. Now these monsters here were jumping in time to it; the good DJ had made it his own. Maybe the DJ was a two-headed

Baltic Belles

monster himself. But with good taste.

Escape into aesthetics was not security, how could it be? From an enjoyable, exciting aesthetic piece you have regarded as your own, you could find yourself looking, at the most unexpected moment, at the plain face of your old antipathy. We know that. The political technologists build up an underground, nationalists listen to Laibach, at a concert by the Arditti Quartet some slacker monster drifts off to a piece of Kagel – how can you keep them away?

You can jump into the fire
But you'll never be free no no

The poet grabbed the pianist by the arm, the beautiful slender arm, of delicious fabric and warm skin, and said: "So, what about it – let's dance!"

"Oh, you know – I'm not, like, on that wavelength. I can't, like, stagger."

"Stuff them – let's go."

"Listen – honestly."

But the girl with the flute was willing.

The poet bawled along with Nilsson and kept on shouting, a proletarian of intellectual work in the midst of the monsters – let them all go to hell!

Her investment-banker classmate waved to her and he waved back.

Oooohooho-aah-aah
We can make each other happy
We can make each other happy
We can make each other happy

She stayed to bawl along with a few numbers, but when she came back, she saw envelopes on the table. "Yes," said the

Baltic Belles

violinist, "the lady of the house had left them." Thirty euros for each of them.

The flautist, sweet little innocent that she was, was dancing with a monster in a pale suit.

The poet saw red.

"I'll fucking tear her apart right here in front of everyone, I fucking will! I'll make a snot-ball of the banknotes, that bloody lady of the manor, bloody little badger-face will get it in the mug! A light blue snot-ball and a red snot-ball will be made out of those banknotes – bloody *thirty euros each*, the bitch!"

The violinist sighed. "I'll talk to her," he said.

The poet took one envelope, pulled out the banknotes, screwed them up and put the envelope back.

"Is that woman around at the moment?" she asked. "And where did our pianist get to?"

"Oh, they went to look at a rare piano." The violinist shrugged. "That... *lady* is still quite out of it, but she was insisting terribly that she wanted to show off her rare instrument. Under the cover of secrecy, I wasn't allowed to go. But to be honest, I'll be going soon," he said.

"Yes," said the poet, "that's what I thought. I'll go and look for them."

In imitation of 18th-century Europe, they had even tried to create a Chinese room here. And a fantasy room, with a chessboard floor, alternating between lemon-sorbet green and white. And real, stuffed swans.

Some waiter or something like that looked at her inquiringly. Toilet? Yeah, I'll find it.

Baltic Belles

Marie-Antoinette, Elisabeth, Charlotte. Hey, hadn't she heard some voices behind the first door?

Marie-Antoinette's door was closed, but next to the door a small staircase led upstairs. Ah, and something she hadn't noticed as she passed: in the stair recess now stood a moderately well-filled Scavenger's Daughter. Well, of course. We are a little threatening, aren't we, we like to make dark spectacles. A romantic imitation of the Middle Ages, that was exactly what they needed. She pulled one of her skirts open. Look, we're driving you on the end of a spike. Ooh! Pathetic. But at least some local joiner maybe got some work.

The room to which the stairs led was draped with deep red velvet. On top of a pseudo-Baroque chest of drawers was a large bone, the poet also noticed, and from one panel of red velvet hung on a chain a shiny new torturer's Pear of Anguish (pathetic, pathetic, pathetic), but behind a nearby partition, she could hear munching, moaning and panting.

They were there on the floor; the lady of the house was crouching by the pianist. The poet stopped to consider whether to step back behind the partition and think what to do next. But look! There was something lying on the dark parquet floor (possibly Magnum Oak Ebony, sixty-one euros fifty per square metre) and there it was. A taser.

The pianist was lying on the floor as if crucified. His mouth was taped shut and his hands and feet were strapped to a silly-looking cross. Aili B. was fussing around beside him and moaning nonsensically, now and then letting out a half-witted chuckle among her moans.

Would the poet know how to use the taser? Might she deal a blow to the wrong person, herself, with it? She knocked the weapon with her foot, so that it slid across the floor under some strange device (a machine from Kafka's penal colony?). Then she grabbed the slender hostess under the shoulders and started tugging her away from the pianist. The drunken estate manager initially put up a strong struggle against her like a little bird, but then let herself go slack and resumed making erotic noises.

"Idiot," said the poet; the lady gave a ghastly sensual laugh and started rolling back and forth on the floor.

The pianist's shirt-front was open, some buttons had been pulled off it, his trouser belt and buttons were also open, but they were not all removed; the lady hadn't had time to undo any more.

The poet looked at the man and he looked back, eyes big and blue as cultured blueberries.

"Oh, shit," said the poet.

"Sorry," she said. She bent over the pianist, and pressed his cheek against her warm cheek. Then she sniffed him. It's best to smell a person's scent from the sides of the nose, between nose and cheek. "Wait, I'll try to... I hope..." murmured the poet, pulling the piece of tape from the pianist's mouth and instead of asking whether the tearing hurt or not, the poet pressed her own mouth in the place of the tape, putting her tongue inside the man's mouth, because she knew it would taste good, and the man let it happen.

Like a miracle, he was another person. Fabric, in its silly sobriety, was covering the most beautiful thing in the world, a human body. The poet opened up the skin-warmed front of the black shirt.

His chest was smooth like a boy's. No tendency to

gynaecomasty, no superfluous feminine mammary muscles, the nipples withdrawn as onto a flat plane. The boyishly smooth chest rose and fell. The poet's hands were a little cool, so that they went through small shocks at the man's body as she moved her fingers down toward the belly. Between the legs he was of course already hard. Like a funny little python it was there under his black boxer-shorts, hot and tough, and now it had to be released. A creature of paradise.

To sleep with you and die.

The poet was pleased that at the last moment she had decided to put on a dress. For events at the manor, where suits and dress with décolletage are worn, she had intended to come in a literary black sweater and jeans. Something had still made her choose a mini-skirt of stretch material, and now she was pleased about it, because when everything necessary had been taken off, it was more comfortable and elegant to straddle her lover, because his aroused member was ready to explode.

The poet looked at the man and he looked back, eyes big and blue as cultured blueberries.

"Oh, shit," said the poet. "Sorry." She bent over the pianist.

Almost painful cascades of heat rushed up from her lower body; she was trying to restrain her panting.

He was a man of the arts, like herself. The lady was wriggling on the floor and groaning; you couldn't work out whether she was expressing a drunk's idea of erotic groans or whether she really felt ill.

The poet wasn't an animal. Of course she was an animal. She starts screaming now, she mustn't throw herself on the pianist. He starts bawling like a beast. She must have had a red halo around her from sheer arousal. Burning cannibalistic desire was puffing out of her nostrils.

But she wasn't allowed to fall into the trap.

It wasn't that the lady was laying a snare for her and she was falling into it, going for somebody of her own kind; and the lady would be looking at them fucking with a giggle, as if it were dog racing.

Did the pianist have a decent boy's grey underpants? That had to be an irreparable loss. What was that frizzy grey called – that grey tone in linen, T-shirts and sweaters – did it have a special name?

The poet smiled nervously, said, "Incredible."

"Sick bitch," the pianist mumbled. His wrist was warm and the strap had rubbed it somewhat red, but not yet chafed it. On the strap was some silly clip or buckle, with which the poet fumbled for a while. No, there was no blood on the wrist; the poet didn't get smeared with it. Another clip came off more easily, and then the man sat up and started flailing his legs to get himself free, but the poet was still bending over his left leg and opening the clip, now quite expertly. A black cotton sock, the ankle. That was all; now she had to withdraw.

As she wallowed on the floor the lady made sounds like squeals; the poet's hands, cool a moment ago, had now gone hot with regret.

Ah, that precipice of physical relations, better than anything else and comfortingly sad! 'I like you and so I want to gobble you up, dive into your flesh, consume it, because I am human. What other limit could I have in relation to another human being? Ah. Darling.'

Like an acid, regret flowed throughout her body.

"Sick bitch," said the pianist again. "She's ripped my shirt apart."

"Did she attack you with the taser?"

"Damn, I don't understand anything. I suppose she did."

"Is everything all right with you?"

The pianist smirked. "I hope so."

"We'll have to call the police."

The lady was still wriggling and mumbling, and the poet was about to yell at her to pull herself together and grow up, when screams were heard, muffled a little by the distance and the walls.

"Look!" cried a shrill female voice. "Look!"

Next came many more screams. *"We're on fire."*

From her drunken worm-like position the lady of the house got to her feet with remarkable speed. Her red shoes remained in the torture chamber.

"What's happening?" said the pianist.

"Should we run?" asked the poet. "We're on the third floor."

When they got down to the corridor, they saw flames across the courtyard. The shingle roof of the coach-house was blazing picturesquely. With renewed hope the poet now put her hand on the pianist's shoulder and slipped it a little way down his upper arm.

"Wow," she said, *"Vot eto daa."*

The pianist did not remove the poet's hand, but when the latter tightened her grip, he said: "Let's go and look."

And as they were walking separately along the corridor, he said: "Well, thank God you came looking for me."

'It could have been the wildest sex in my life,' thought the poet. 'I'm inhibited, uncreative.'

When they got to the hall, the shingle roof was totally ablaze. The disco had stopped, people were standing below the windows, the administrator was hauling out a long hose with a couple of helpers, a few chaps were watching helplessly with a fire extinguisher in the yard. The Lamborghini had been driven further away, and probably a few more cars.

The poet found some untouched pepper-cheese balls on one table. She took them to the pianist, put her hand on his back, still with some kind of hope, and said: "We must talk to the police. About that taser. And that stuff. They'll come here anyway with the fire brigade, investigating and taking statements."

"She got her punishment."

"It's criminal."

"It is."

"You'll have to make a statement."

"Listen, I'd better not just now. Honestly."

"What?"

The police didn't find the taser. In the little red room where the poet had led them nothing illegal was found. Of course they didn't have a warrant for a search, nor were there any victims who would have claimed that a weapon was used on them, but Mrs. Aili B. was quite happy to show them the room, and under those ridiculous prickly installations, for which no police order could be made, let alone a confiscation, nothing was found lying around. Poets of today often lack existential experience, you see. Their gaze is directed inwards or into books. The question is whether they would recognise a taser.

The inspector said nothing.

If it hadn't been dark and if they had looked backward as they left the manor park, they would have seen the wall of the garage-gallery seeming to split into two, and what was left of the scorched rafters of the shingle roof falling with a doleful rustle into the duck pond. "Undoubtedly," said the poet, "undoubtedly."

Yet for quite a while she was kept awake at night by dismay and regret, thinking about that man, tied up, delicious, gifted, waiting to be exploited. For there was clearly an invitation in the man's gaze. So sweet, natural and fluent it would have been; they would have drunk champagne in a café the next evening and laughed about Estonian culture, the culture of Estonia, and the poet would have been allowed to run her hand down the man's shirt. Everything would have changed.

And the poet thought: 'An egg is what I am, the last egg. The last bear. I didn't understand that this drunken woman was simply a tool of a benevolent fate.'

'Fate doesn't exist; it consists of my own clumsy stumblings, flatness. As you sow, you reap, and so forth.'

And then she thought: 'It was pure respect and nobility, for the sake of another person I overcame temptation, and that was the only thinkable thing. Anything else would have been vulgar and lacking in style, because everything that happens on an unequal basis is vulgar and lacking in style, and you can't go on living with vulgarity.'

And the poet saw life as empty and interesting as she always did, but it was to be a long time before her regret retreated. And even a few months afterwards the memory could come rushing back, and then the poet was forced to think: 'Noble. Obtuse. Noble. Obtuse. Noble. Obtuse. Noble. Grey, the underpants must have been grey.'

2014

Translated by Christopher Moseley

Dedalus Celebrating Women's Literature 2018–2028

In 2018 Dedalus began celebrating the centenary of women getting the vote in the UK with a programme of women's fiction. In 1918, Parliament passed an act granting the vote to women over the age of 30 who were householders, the wives of householders, occupiers of property with an annual rent of £5, and graduates of British universities. About 8.4 million women gained the vote. It was a big step forward but it was not until the Equal Franchise Act of 1928 that women over 21 were able to vote and women finally achieved the same voting rights as men. This act increased the number of women eligible to vote to 15 million. Dedalus' aim is to publish six titles each year, most of which will be translations from other European languages, for the next ten years as we commemorate this important milestone.

Titles published so far:

The Prepper Room by Karen Duve
Take Six: Six Portuguese Women Writers edited by Margaret Jull Costa
Slav Sisters: The Dedalus Book of Russian Women's Literature edited by Natasha Perova
Baltic Belles: The Dedalus Book of Estonian Women's Literature edited by Elle-Mari Talivee
The Madwoman of Serrano by Dina Salústio

Forthcoming titles include:

Baltic Belles: The Dedalus Book of Latvian Women's Literature edited by Eva Eglaja
The Price of Dreams by Margherita Giacobino
Cleopatra goes to Prison by Claudia Durastanti
Venice Noir by Isabella Panfido
The Girl from the Sea and other Stories by Sophia de Mello Breyner Andresen
Fair Trade Heroin by Rachael McGill
Primordial Soup by Christine Leunens
The Medusa Child by Sylvie Germain

The Ruddles   Parody
   Ruttles   re: Beatles
 all you need is Cart